DOUBLE JEOPARDY

BOOKS BY STUART WOODS

FICTION

Double Jeopardy*

Hush-Hush*

Shakeup*

Choppy Water*

Hit List*

Treason*

Stealth*

Contraband*

Wild Card*

A Delicate Touch*

Desperate Measures*

Turbulence*

Shoot First*

Unbound*

Quick & Dirty*

Indecent Exposure*

Fast & Loose*

Below the Belt*

Sex, Lies & Serious Money*

Dishonorable Intentions*

Family Jewels*

Scandalous Behavior*

Foreign Affairs*

Naked Greed*

Hot Pursuit*

Insatiable Appetites*

Paris Match*

Cut and Thrust*

Carnal Curiosity*

Standup Guy*

Doing Hard Time*

Unintended Consequences*

Collateral Damage*

Severe Clear*

Unnatural Acts*

D.C. Dead*

Son of Stone*

Bel-Air Dead*

Strategic Moves*

Santa Fe Edge†

Lucid Intervals*

Kisser*

Hothouse Orchid‡

Loitering with Intent*

Mounting Fears§

Hot Mahogany*

Santa Fe Dead†

Beverly Hills Dead

Shoot Him If He Runs*

Fresh Disasters*

Short Straw†

Dark Harbor*

Iron Orchid‡

Two-Dollar Bill*

The Prince of Beverly Hills

Reckless Abandon*

Capital Crimes§

Dirty Work*

Blood Orchid‡

The Short Forever*

Orchid Blues‡
Cold Paradise*
L.A. Dead*
The Run§
Worst Fears Realized*
Orchid Beach‡
Swimming to Catalina*
Dead in the Water*
Dirt*
Choke
Imperfect Strangers
Heat
Dead Eyes
L.A. Times
Santa Fe Rules†
New York Dead*
Palindrome
Grass Roots§
White Cargo
Deep Lie§

Under the Lake
Run Before the Wind§
Chiefs§

COAUTHORED BOOKS

Bombshell** (with Parnell Hall)
Skin Game** (with Parnell Hall)
The Money Shot**
   (with Parnell Hall)
Barely Legal†† (with Parnell Hall)
Smooth Operator**
   (with Parnell Hall)

TRAVEL

A Romantic's Guide to the Country
   Inns of Britain and Ireland (1979)

MEMOIR

Blue Water, Green Skipper

*A Stone Barrington Novel
†An Ed Eagle Novel
‡A Holly Barker Novel
§A Will Lee Novel
**A Teddy Fay Novel
††A Herbie Fisher Novel

DOUBLE JEOPARDY

STUART WOODS

G. P. PUTNAM'S SONS

NEW YORK

PUTNAM
— EST. 1838 —

G. P. PUTNAM'S SONS
Publishers Since 1838
An imprint of Penguin Random House LLC
penguinrandomhouse.com

Hardcover ISBN 9780593188385
E-book ISBN 9780593188408

Printed in the United States of America
1 3 5 7 9 10 8 6 4 2

BOOK DESIGN BY KATY RIEGEL

This is a work of fiction. Names, characters, places, and incidents either are
the product of the author's imagination or are used fictitiously, and any
resemblance to actual persons, living or dead, businesses, companies,
events, or locales is entirely coincidental.

DOUBLE JEOPARDY

1

tone Barrington walked into his office on a Monday
morning and found three pink memo slips, saying
that a John Keegan had called and needed to see him ur-
gently.

Joan Robertson, his secretary, came into the room without being asked, and said, "No, I don't know who he is. He's
been leaving messages on the machine since early this
morning."

"Perhaps you know why there's no number to call back
on these slips?"

"Oh, I just thought I'd make life more difficult for you.
Isn't that my job?"

"I'm just asking."

"I can only write down the messages left," she said. "If

there had been a number, I would have written that down, too. If past performance is any indication, he'll call back."

"I can't argue with that," Stone said. His phone rang. Joan picked it up.

"The Barrington Practice at Woodman & Weld," she said. "Ah, yes, Mr. Keegan, I have him right here." She handed Stone the phone with a triumphant grin.

"Good morning, this is Stone Barrington."

"Thank God," Keegan said. "My name is John Keegan, call me Jack. I need to speak to you in person as soon as possible."

"Where are you, Jack?"

"In a cab, on the way in from the airport."

"A New York airport?"

"Sorry, yes. LaGuardia. I just got off the shuttle from Boston."

"Do you have my address?"

Keegan spoke it to him.

"May I know what this is about?"

"I'll tell you when I see you. Suffice to say, it's a family matter."

"I'll be available when you get here. I hope you brought your raincoat and galoshes." But Keegan had hung up. It was pouring outside.

A few minutes later, the office doorbell rang. Stone's office was in a former dentist's office in a house that he had inherited from a great-aunt many years before and remodeled. He heard the sounds of an umbrella closing and outer clothing being shucked off.

Joan stuck her head in. "Mr. Keegan to see you," she said, "slightly damp."

Keegan walked in wearing a good suit and a necktie, and carrying an old-fashioned briefcase, stuffed. He dropped it on the floor with a *thump* and offered his hand.

Stone shook it and waved him to a seat. "I expect you could use some hot coffee," Stone said.

"Oh, yes."

"How?" Joan asked.

"Black, please."

"It's strong. Do you want it weaker?"

"Strong is good."

She left and returned with a steaming mug and set it on a small table beside him. He sipped it gratefully.

"You said this was a family matter," Stone said. "I have only one family member, a son, Peter, who lives in Los Angeles. Is this about him?"

"No, sorry. The other side of the family." He handed a card over: "Keegan, Kay, and Williams, Boston."

"And you're Keegan," Stone said. "Just a wild guess."

"I and my father before me. All three of us partners had fathers who preceded us in the firm."

"Neat and tidy. The other side of the family? The Stones?"

"Yes."

"They're all dead, except two of them, who are . . . unavailable."

"Mr. Barrington . . ."

"Call me Stone."

"Stone . . ." He hesitated.

"Yes?"

"I'm new to this case, and it would be helpful to me if you could recount your knowledge of your Stone relatives, particularly with regard to your residence on Islesboro."

"How far back do you want me to go?"

"Grandparents."

"My mother, Matilda, was a Stone. She and my father, a Barrington, were both from western Massachusetts, both families in the weaving business, mostly men's suitings. My parents fell in love as teenagers; she was studying art at Mount Holyoke and he, law, at Yale. Her parents objected to the pairing."

"On what grounds?"

"My father had leftist political views. He had even joined the Communist Party for a brief time, mostly to annoy *his* father, I think. They married anyway—eloped. As a result, they were both banished from their families: he for his politics, she for marrying him."

"Did you have any cousins on the Stone side?"

"Two first cousins, Caleb and Richard."

"Did you know them well?"

"Not until, at eighteen, I was invited to spend a summer on Islesboro with them, during a brief thaw in family relations."

"And how did you get on with them?"

"Splendidly, with Dick, poorly with Caleb, who was both a bully and an ass, as bullies usually are. I finally had occasion to punch him in the nose, earning the displeasure of his mother, who thereafter declared me persona non grata on the island. I was not invited back."

"Did you see them after that?"

"I saw Dick once, when he came to New York on business. We had dinner and renewed our warm friendship. That was the last time I saw him."

"Did you communicate on any sort of regular basis?"

"Not really. I never met his wife."

"And did the Stone brothers have progeny?"

"Dick and his wife had a daughter. Caleb, twin sons."

"Did you ever hear from Dick again?"

"I received a package from him, with a letter instructing me to put it in my safe and to open it only in the event of his death."

"What happened after that?"

"He died."

"Murdered, along with his wife and child, I am informed."

"You are correctly informed."

"Did you learn who killed them?"

"I deduced who did. The law did not."

"What was your deduction?"

"That Enos and Eben Stone murdered all three, along with a number of local, Boston, and New Haven women. Oh, and both their parents. I believe the twins are serving life without possibility of parole in the state prison."

"That is not quite correct," Keegan said.

"How not so?"

"The Stone twins confessed to the killing of their parents, pled guilty, and were sentenced to life."

"What about no parole?"

"Their first parole hearing is the day after tomorrow."

2

S tone blinked. "Whatever happened to 'without parole'?"

"Like you, the police deduced that the Stone twins were guilty of all the aforementioned murders, but they did not have the evidence to prove their guilt beyond a reasonable doubt. In shooting their parents, however, they were careless, and the prosecution had them cold."

"Wasn't that good enough for life without parole?"

"It should have been, but two factors intervened: first, the boys claimed, convincingly, that their father had sexually abused them as children and that their mother knew about it but did nothing. Second, the state was deeply embarrassed about its failure to charge them on all counts, and they just wanted the case to go away. So, aided by a clever attorney—my father—they pled guilty to the murders of their parents, in exchange for life with the possibility of parole, something the prosecution thought never would happen."

"And you," Stone said. "Are you telling me all this because of the guilt of your father's participation?"

"Yes. I tried to talk him out of it, but he thought it would be a feather in his cap. As a result, he was asked to resign from his clubs, and he never took another criminal case. Also, the twins were a couple of years behind me at school, and I had always thought they were evil little shits. My great regret is that Maine got rid of the death penalty in the 1870s."

"All right, we're both up to date, I think," Stone said. "Now tell me why we are telling each other all this."

"I can't very well show up at the parole hearing and beg the board to deny."

"Why not?"

"Because it would further humiliate my father to oppose him in a case that has already caused him such pain. He loved his clubs, and he is quite old now and has already had one stroke."

"So, you'd like me to appear and plead the case against parole?"

"If you would be so kind; I would be very grateful."

"And have you been able to come up with any convincing evidence for me to present?"

"I fear I have not."

"Let me guess: the twins have been ideal prisoners and they charmed all they have met."

"That's about the size of it."

"So, I'm supposed to appear at the hearing and tell the board that, contrary to all the available evidence, they are very bad boys, not to mention evil little shits, and they should throw away the key."

"Sort of," Keegan admitted.

"And, of course, the twins will have a parade of other witnesses—guards, nurses, fellow prisoners, and, let's not forget, the prison doctor, who will all swear to their cuddliness."

"You make it sound hopeless," Keegan said, his shoulders slumping into his damp suit.

"I don't make it sound hopeless," Stone said. "It *is* hopeless."

"Will you, at least, come up to Maine for the hearing and share my bench with me, holding a briefcase? That would make it appear that I'm not alone in all this."

"Jack," Stone said, not unkindly. "Apart from your father, do you have any family?"

Keegan shook his head. "My wife and I were childless, and she died last year."

"Well, my advice to you is to pack up your shingle and your bags and retire to some remote place in a distant land, but not without a shotgun handy, because your appearance before the parole board, no matter how ineffective, is not going to win the affections of the Stone twins, and they will not have short memories."

Keegan sighed. "I had hoped to avoid retirement."

"Why avoid it? Many men of your age retire every day, sitting under a palm tree and drinking piña coladas."

"My problem is, I love the law, love practicing it every day."

"Do you play golf?"

"Sadly, no."

"Time to take it up," Stone said brightly. He rose. "I wish I could help, Jack. I really do, but I have no argument to make that would not just make things worse for both of us."

"I understand," Keegan said, standing and offering his hand. "Thank you for hearing me out."

"One thing might help," Stone said.

"What's that?"

"Don't appear. I think we both understand that your absence would not make a difference in the outcome, and the twins will be grateful, not vengeful, whenever they hear the Keegan name, as long as it's your father they're thinking of."

"You have a point," Keegan said.

"Check into a good hotel, see a show or two, get drunk, and be in another state when the board meets."

Joan helped him into his soggy rainwear and put him out onto the street with a cheery wave.

3

Stone didn't have to look up the number. He dialed the Dark Harbor Shop, in the village of the same name, on Islesboro, Maine.

"This is Billy." Billy Hotchkiss was the cousin of Stone's Maine property manager, Seth Hotchkiss, the owner of the Dark Harbor Shop, and the fount of all knowledge about the island and its inhabitants. He was also, among other things, the only real estate broker on the island.

"Billy, it's Stone Barrington. How are you?"

"Well, Stone," Billy said, "after your most recent visit, if gun brass was gold, I'd be sitting under a palm tree somewhere, sipping piña coladas. But never mind; picking it up gives the kids something to do with their afternoons."

"I'm sorry about the shootout, Billy. Please tell everybody

that. But I was on the wrong end of it, and it was coming fast."

"That part we got. Listen, I'm glad you called, I've got some news. Mr. Greco and his family have decided the island isn't right for them, and they're putting the Stone house back on the market. I've already got an offer, it fell into my hands not ten minutes ago," Billy said. "It's from a shelter corporation, since the bidders don't want people to know who they are."

Stone took Billy's meaning.

"But you and I know who they are, don't we, Billy?"

"Well, *I* know who they are. I'm not so sure about you."

"Let me put it this way, Billy: How much would I have to offer to make the present owner forget he had another offer?"

"You should've asked me what the offer was. I'd have told you that."

"How much was the offer, Billy?"

"Three million dollars, with the house, the boathouse, the new guesthouse, and six point two acres of prime waterfront. I'm sure the owner would like to get a little something out of it for his trouble."

"Would three and a half million get it off the market?"

"Well, I'm just guessing here, but you're fucking right it would."

"Well, then, you fax me a legal definition of the property and all the usual stuff, and I'll fax you a signed offer before noon—all cash, condition as is, closing Friday at noon. I'll wire you three hundred and fifty grand of earnest money. And you and the wife can dine out grandly this evening on your commission."

"I'll call up Mr. Greco, and get his verbal approval, before I put us to all that trouble."

"All right. You can tell him I'm the buyer, if you like, but not why I'm buying."

"Well, you haven't told *me* why you're buying, have you?" Billy said.

"No. But we both know, don't we?"

"You can assume that."

"Let's get it done before that corporate buyer hears about it, shall we?"

"All right by me."

"Call me if there are any problems. But let's not have any problems, okay?"

"Avoiding problems is my life's work," Billy said, and they both hung up.

Stone buzzed Joan.

"Yes, sir?"

"In about a minute, you're going to get a fax about a house in Dark Harbor from Billy Hotchkiss. When it comes in, transfer the relevant information on it to a boilerplate offer, and print it out for my signature and your notarizing. Also, wire transfer three hundred and fifty grand to Billy's real estate office account as earnest money. Got that?"

"Yes, but let me be sure I've got it right: you're buying yet *another* property. This one in a place where you *already* own a house?"

"That is correct, and I don't have time to explain why. We just need to get that offer into Billy's hands fast. And call Charley Fox at Triangle Investments and tell him to find another three million somewhere in my checking account, because we're closing before noon on Friday. Oh, and I'll need a cashier's check for the three million in Billy's hands on Thursday, and make my attorney of record Herbie Fisher. And print me a power of attorney for Ed Rawls to act for me at the closing, and send that to Billy, too."

"Mine is not to reason why," Joan muttered on her way out.

"Keep thinking that!" Stone shouted after her.

Stone called his old NYPD partner, Dino Bacchetti, now New York City's police commissioner.

"Bacchetti."

"We need to have dinner tonight," Stone said, "because my news won't wait any longer than that."

"Here's an idea," Dino said. "Let's have dinner. Viv is out of town, of course."

"Seven at Patroon."

"Yep." Dino hung up.

Joan buzzed. "Billy Hotchkiss on one."

"Thanks, and book me at Patroon, two at seven." Stone pressed the button. "Hey, Billy."

"Hey, yourself. I talked to Greco about your offer."

"What'd he say?"

"He said to throw a net over you before you can get away."

"You do that. I'm giving Ed Rawls a power of attorney to represent me at the closing, and you'll have a wire transfer for three million and change on Thursday."

"I wish all my clients were as decisive as you," Billy said, then hung up.

4

Stone got to Patroon first, ordered a drink, and phoned Ed Rawls.

"Speak to me."

"Ed, it's Stone. I've just signed a power of attorney for you."

"Do I get *all* your money?"

"No, you just get to show up at the Dark Harbor Shop on Friday morning and sign all the documents for me to buy the Stone property." Stone filled Ed in on what he'd learned from Jack Keegan about the Stone twins' upcoming parole.

"You beat the boys to the punch?"

"By a whisker."

"My recollection of the twins tells me they are not going to react kindly to the news."

"It's their fault for not getting their offer in soon enough."

"Tell me, where do two convicts get the money to buy such a place?"

"From their grandmother's estate. She died before they plead guilty, and they came into something like sixty mil."

"Then they're more dangerous than ever."

"If they get paroled in a couple of days."

"How are you going to prevent that?"

"I have two plans: one, I have no idea. Two, if that doesn't work, I'll try to see that they violate parole and are stuck back inside promptly."

"I prefer plan two."

"I prefer plan one, which involves preventing them from being paroled."

"How are you going to do that?"

"I told you, I don't know. Yet. I'm having dinner with Dino right now, and I'm going to let him worry about it. Good evening." He hung up as Dino slid into the booth. They got him a drink.

"Now, let me tell you everything that's happened." Stone launched into a recap. When he finished, he said, "Your turn."

Dino pointed a thumb at himself. "*My* turn? Are you speaking to me?"

"Directly to you."

"What do you expect from me?"

"I expect you to tell me how to get the parole of the Stone twins denied. After that, you can tell me how to get them killed in prison."

Dino cupped a hand behind an ear. "Sorry, I didn't get that, and I don't want to not hear it again."

"You're a big help."

Dino took a sheet of paper from his inside pocket and unfolded it. "Actually, I heard about this earlier today, and . . ."

"And you didn't call me?"

"By that time, you already knew about it."

"What's on the paper?"

"I called a guy I know who had been seriously intimate with a woman who works at the Maine State Prison. He got her to scan and send a copy of their prison record to him. Here's a summary of what he learned. Forgive me if I paraphrase."

"Granted."

"Okay, since the day the twins were incarcerated they have been perfectly ideal prisoners, every warden's dream. They didn't get into fights, because they're big, muscular guys, and they watched each other's backs. They cheerfully performed any task they were ordered to, including serving at the warden's dinner parties. They taught other prisoners to read. They wrote pardon requests and appeals for other prisoners. Did I mention that they had already graduated from Yale Law when they were arrested, and subsequently requested and got permission to take the Maine bar exam? They were driven to the test site by two prison guards, and now they can practice law. There was a move afoot to have their licenses yanked, which has not yet succeeded. After a year in max, they were transferred to the hospital wing, where they were made very comfortable."

"How'd they swing that?" Stone asked.

"If I had to guess, I would guess that palms were crossed with silver, but who knows? May I continue?"

"Please."

"They reorganized the prison library, replaced the out-of-date law books with new ones, and paid for a computer link to a legal website for research, endearing them to the warden. They were pretty much running a law firm out of the prison library."

"Didn't the warden know they were homicidal maniacs?"

"I must point out that they were convicted only of murdering their parents, and their testimony about their dad's sexual abuse of the boys won them friends. Among them, a young woman who started a get-the-twins-out movement, which has a big following on the Internet.

Stone started to speak, but Dino held up a hand.

"Let me finish. The prison psychiatrist examined them both at length and came to know them well. His opinion is that they are brilliant, charming, and saner than you or I, but with a touch of narcissism. He also noted that they are the most identical identical twins he has ever seen. He persuaded them to get visible tattoos, so the staff could tell them apart—a plus sign on Eben's left earlobe and a minus sign on Enos's."

"That's convenient."

"He also says that they seem to think and act as one man. Their interpersonal communications seem almost telepathic."

Dino sat back and sipped his drink. "Got all that?"

"Yes."

"So what's your best idea?"

"Let's talk about how to get them killed in prison," Stone said.

5

Dino accepted another Scotch, while shaking his head. "That's not going to happen."

"Why not?" Stone asked. "You can have anybody killed in prison."

"The boys are six-three, two hundred ten pounds; they're not muscle-bound, because they're not weight lifters. They spar, they wrestle, and they hit each other with Japanese sticks. They're lithe and, as I say, there are two of them. The whole prison population is scared shitless of them. That makes them shiv-proof."

"Don't they have any weaknesses?"

"Not unless you include batshit crazy."

"You said the psychiatrist said they are sane."

"Yeah, but they're smart enough to fool him."

"So, you're saying we can't touch them."

"No," Dino replied. "We can get them. It's just that so far we don't have a clue in hell how to do that."

"There must be a way."

"Well, you could keep pissing them off, until they try to kill you, then shoot them. But there's always the risk that they'll get lucky. Still, you've made a good start, buying the family property out from under them. You did buy it under a corporate name, didn't you?"

"Well, ah . . ."

"Oh, shit."

"It was all so rushed. The contract and the earnest money have already gone out. I'll get it changed in the morning."

"Good idea. It might take them a few minutes to figure out who bought it—*if* Billy Hotchkiss can keep his mouth shut, a quality for which he is not personally known."

"God, this is depressing." Stone moaned.

"Clinically depressing, or just sad?"

"Just sad."

"How's Rocky?" Dino asked. Rocky Hardwick, a recent companion of Stone's and a CIA officer, had been wounded in an attack on his Maine house.

"She's good. She's gone down to Virginia, to recuperate at her mother's house."

"In an ambulance, I hope."

"In a medivac chopper, with a doctor and a nurse along for company."

"Do you think she blames you for getting shot?"

"I hope not. But who could blame her for blaming me?"

"She should blame Lance Cabot. He's her boss, and he sent her to you about that computer thing, when they tried to extort dough out of you."

"I like that idea, but it's hard to suggest it to her at this distance."

"Send her some flowers with a note saying, 'This is all Lance's fault.'"

"The flowers are a good idea, but I don't know about the blame. I think that, in her mind, she's already fixed it. I just don't know where."

They ordered the chateaubriand for two. It had just been served when Lance Cabot walked in and sat down. "That looks good," he said, taking one of Dino's forks and stabbing a chunk.

"Order some," Dino said, moving the serving dish away from Lance's reach.

"The usual," Lance said to a waiter.

"The usual what, Mr. Cabot?"

"The usual martini and the usual Caesar salad and the usual strip steak, medium rare. And the usual haricots verts and fried onion rings.

"So," Lance continued, stealing a slice of beef from Stone's plate, "what are you going to do about the twins?"

"I was hoping you'd have some thoughts on that," Stone said.

Dino handed Lance his folded sheet of paper. "Here's a summary of their prison file."

"I've already read the whole thing," Lance said, brushing Dino's paper away disdainfully with the back of his hand. "Discouraging, isn't it?"

"That's what Stone was just saying."

"Don't be discouraged, Stone," Lance said.

"Why not?" Stone asked.

"There's always a way."

"What's the way this time?"

"Well, you could hire Ed Rawls for the job. He might even give you his two-for-one rate."

"My relationship with Ed is one of friendship, not hired killing."

"He's the only man I know who could take them out with one bullet through both heads."

"As attractive as you make that sound, I'm not going to take that route."

"Your decision, if you wish to shorten your own life."

"Why would they want to kill me?"

"Maybe because you chased them down at the airport and blocked their takeoff until the police arrived."

"Well, there is that," Stone admitted. "That, and I just bought the Stone house in Maine out from under them."

"I hope you used a corporate name."

Stone winced. "That will be taken care of first thing tomorrow morning."

"Don't oversleep."

Lance's dinner arrived, and he set about catching up with Stone and Dino.

"Lance," Dino said, "how is it you always know everything?"

"I employ thousands of field agents to keep me informed." Lance was the director of the Central Intelligence Agency.

"Even in Maine?"

"*Everywhere.*"

"How can we stop the Stone twins from being paroled?" Stone asked.

"I don't know," Lance said. "What I do know is, it doesn't matter if they're not paroled."

"Why not?"

"Because the newly seated governor of their state has already told his intimates that he's going to pardon them, if they're not paroled."

"Why would the governor want to do that?"

"Two reasons: One, because he was at Yale with Caleb Stone, the boys' father, his best friend, and, incidentally, your first cousin. And two, because he can, and he would do anything for his friend's boys."

"I've always thought that was a lousy reason to do things," Stone said.

"Be that as it may," Lance said.

6

Stone had finished breakfast in bed and was working on the *Times* crossword, trying not to think about the Stone twins, when his phone rang. He recognized the Virginia number immediately.

"Hello, there," he said with enthusiasm.

"Hello, yourself," Rocky replied.

"How goes your recovery?"

"Slowly. It's rehab five days a week, and it hurts when I do that."

"You have to, if you want a working body," he advised.

"I know, and I will."

"How's your mom doing?"

"Not as well as I. Her drugs don't work anymore. Her doctor won't tell me how long she's got, but a doctor friend tells me only a few weeks. As he put it, 'Life is a river, and your mother has hit a waterfall.' All they can do is keep her out of pain. It looks like I'll be well just about the time she goes."

"I'm sorry to hear that. I lost both my parents a long while back. They pretty much took care of each other, until Dad died, then she didn't last long."

"She's still trying to take care of me," Rocky said. "She's making soup right now."

"Do you miss work?"

"Funny you should mention that. Lance called me yesterday, told me to take my time and then . . ."

She didn't finish the sentence. "And then, what?"

"He offered me a new job, running a department."

"Good! What department?"

"Legislative affairs—liaising with Congress, both houses."

"That sounds like a great leap forward," Stone said, but he was feeling less enthusiastic than he was trying to seem.

"It's a D.C. job, of course. I couldn't handle it from New York. I don't suppose you'd like to live in D.C.?"

Stone didn't hesitate. "Good guess." He'd already been offered a very nice position in D.C. and turned it down, in spite of the free house and limo service. And he couldn't imagine living in the same city with both Holly and Rocky. "Are you going to accept his offer?"

"I already have," Rocky said, "if with some big regrets."

"I appreciate the compliment."

"Mom still has the family apartment in Dupont Circle,

so I'll redo it and move in there when . . . when we're done here."

"So you won't be coming back to New York?"

"No. I'm listing my apartment with a broker today."

Oh, the finality of it, he said to himself.

"I'm going to work very hard at not missing you," she said. "Goodbye, Stone."

"Bye-bye, Rocky." She hung up first.

Stone decided to feel sorry for himself until noon, then shake it off.

The phone rang again. "Good morning, Dino," he said. "A little early for you, isn't it?"

"I got a speech to make in L.A., and Viv is going to fly in from Hong Kong to meet me there."

"Use my house," Stone said.

"Hey, there's an idea! I wish I'd thought of that."

"I'll call the Arrington and tell them to staff up. You can have Ben and Peter and the wives over for dinner." These were their two sons.

"Why don't you and Rocky fly out and meet us?"

"You're just looking for a free ride. And Rocky has accepted a new job from Lance, running legislative affairs for the Agency."

"Oops! No more New York nights, huh?"

"You guessed it."

"Well, it's early. You've got all day to look for a dinner date."

"I was going to ask you to fly up to Maine with me and for both of us to testify at the parole hearing."

"Who, me? Maine? I run the NYPD, remember? I don't meddle in other law enforcement departments, especially in other states. And anyway, I'm going to be luxuriating in a big, comfortable house in Bel-Air."

"How long are you staying?"

"At least until you get back from Maine, without your head, which will be handed to you."

"Thanks for the encouragement. It means an awful lot."

"My advice is more important: take a pass on this one, and don't get the attention of those boys."

"I've had worse advice," Stone said. "Come to think of it, I've had worse advice from you."

"Have a nice time," Dino said. "I'm certainly going to." He hung up.

Stone, showered and dressed, went down to his office, and Joan popped in.

"Good morning," he said. "Please call the L.A. Arrington and let them know Dino and Viv are flying in. She's arriving from Hong Kong. Find out the flight numbers from Dino, and have the hotel meet them and take them to my house. Also, ask them to staff up for a few days. They can ask Dino how long."

"Will you be going to Maine tomorrow?" Joan asked.

"I'll let you know later."

She left. He picked up the phone and called the Maine State Police in Augusta and asked for Sergeant Young.

"Tom Young."

"Hi, Tom, it's Stone Barrington."

There was a long pause, then: "I'll call you back on another line in five minutes. Don't mention any names." He hung up.

Stone tapped his foot for seven minutes, then his cell rang.

"Tom?"

"Goddamnit, I told you, no names!"

"Sorry, that was clumsy of me."

"Tell me why you're calling, not that I don't know."

"You know about . . . the hearing?"

"Of course, I do."

"I had a thought that you and I might attend and give our personal views on other crimes they committed, and . . ."

"Stop right there."

Stone stopped.

"Let me be as clear as I can about this: my boss is retiring in a few weeks, and I want his job. Under the past governor I'd have been a shoo-in. But although the new governor and I have a pleasant relationship, there's no certainty that he'll pick me."

"I understand, but . . ."

"Let me finish."

Stone shut up.

"His views about the subjects of the hearing are well-known, to the extent that, if the board should deny parole, he'll issue a pardon. If I buck him on this, it's a certainty that I'll be passed over for the promotion. That job is all I've ever wanted."

"I do understand," Stone said. "Do you have any advice on how I should proceed?"

"Yes. First, don't show up at the hearing. If you decide to do so anyway, don't ask me for advice on how to proceed. Clear?"

"Clear. Thanks, anyway."

"You have nothing to thank me for." Young hung up.

Stone started thinking again, then he made another call.

7

Stone dialed the Dark Harbor Shop, on Islesboro.

"Billy speaking."

"Billy, it's Stone."

"Stone, I got word from Joan your paperwork and funds are en route. We'll close at ten on Friday morning."

"That's fine, Billy, but I called about something else."

"I was afraid of that."

"You don't know what that is."

"Let me guess: you've run out of options on influencing the parole board. But now it has occurred to you that two of the women raped and murdered by the Stone twins were among our summer people. Now you want to involve me in that. Well, I don't have anything to testify about, so I'm not going to testify about it."

"I don't want you to testify, Billy."

"You don't?"

"You don't have any knowledge of those events."

"Only what I hear, and I hear a lot. What is it you want?"

"Do you believe that the Stone twins raped and murdered those two women?"

"With all my heart and soul, which is to say, none of that would be useful to the board."

"I understand that. That's why—"

"Wait a minute, I think I know what's on your mind."

"Do you want to tell me, or the other way around?"

"Those two women had husbands and children."

"Right."

"You want the husbands to testify that they believe that the twins murdered their wives."

"Something like that."

"Let me tell you why they'll never do that."

"All right, tell me."

"The husband of the first victim has remarried, and his kids are too young to remember anything about their mother's death."

"You can stop right there," Stone said. "What about the other husband? Has he remarried?"

"No, but he's engaged to a woman who is a lot richer than he is, and his kids are old enough to remember their mother and how she died. He's not going to want to fuck up his life or theirs."

"Got it," Stone said.

"There's another reason why nobody would testify, even if they had certain knowledge of the events."

"Which is?"

"I don't know if you remember, but a gossip rag got ahold of the murder-scene photographs, and they were, shall we say, graphic."

"I didn't know that."

"Well, everybody else on this island does. And nobody wants to end up posing for pictures like that."

Stone sighed. "Well, I guess I can't argue with them."

"No, you can't. And you ought to give some thought to what's going to happen when the Stone boys learn who bought their family house out from under them."

"I've taken precautions. The buyer is a Delaware corporation, and they can't penetrate that."

"Well, that's exactly what I'm going to tell them, when they get around to asking. And they will."

"Good idea, Billy."

"I expect you know that I keep a forty-five automatic stashed under my cash register."

"Everybody knows that, Billy."

"Well, I've added a sawed-off shotgun to my little armory, and I don't care who knows it."

"I'll be sure and mention that to the twins, when they come to see me."

"Just you remember that those boys are wicked clever,

with the emphasis on 'wicked.' And you might not see them coming."

"I'll keep that in mind."

"My story is that the buyers are a family from down south, and they don't know anybody here. The only person I've talked to about the house is a lawyer from Savannah, and he doesn't know who they are either, just that they like their privacy."

"That sounds good to me."

"Are you coming up here to close the sale, Stone?"

"No, Ed Rawls will stand in for me. He can sign everything, then I'll release the funds."

"Good, I hope it works. Is that all, Stone?"

"That's all, Billy."

Billy hung up.

Stone checked off the boxes in his brain. He was all out of options.

8

Stone was at his desk on Friday morning when Joan came in.

"I've got both Billy Hotchkiss and Ed Rawls on line one," she said.

Stone punched the speaker button. "Good morning, gentlemen."

"Good morning, yourself," Billy said.

"Yeah, yeah," Rawls grumbled.

"Everything okay?"

"That's why we called," Billy said. "Ed has signed and initialed everything. Now all we need is money, and the Stone property is yours."

"Joan?" He knew she'd still be on the line.

"I await your instructions," she replied.

"Send the rest of the money now."

"The bank is standing by. Hold for a moment." She got off the line, and another lit up on Stone's desk phone. "What else is going on up there?"

"The hearing has started in Belfast," Rawls said. "You want to watch?"

"How would I do that?"

"Well, I don't know, but I believe Joan can figure it out. It's streaming, live."

Stone barely knew what that meant. "When we're done with the money, tell her about it, will you?"

"Sure. And don't worry about their seeing you. It's a one-way thing."

Joan came back on the line. "The funds are winging their way. I figure they're within sight of Penobscot Bay right now."

"My banker will call when they are perched on his windowsill," Billy said.

"Joan," Stone said. "Ed is going to give you some info about streaming. Will you see if you can get it done?"

"Sure. I'll call him on his cell." She clicked off.

Stone heard another phone ringing at the other end, then another.

"Okay," Billy said. "We have received the funds. You're the proud owner of a large, white elephant."

"Thanks so much," Stone said. "I'll hang up now and place myself in the hands of Ed and Joan. Thanks for your help, Billy."

"Thanks for the sale, Stone."

"Oh, something else: Is there someone on the island who decorates houses nicely, or do I have to go to Camden?"

"There is an excellent interior designer in residence here," Billy said. "Her name is Tracey Hotchkiss. Would you like her number?"

"Any relation?"

"She has the good fortune to be married to me," Billy replied.

"Well, tell her she has an assignment."

"You want to talk to her about style?"

"Have her go over to my house. Seth will let her in. That should give her an idea. Tell her she can spend half a million dollars. And I want everything: furniture, pictures, sheets, towels, rugs, kitchen stuff, the works. Tell her I want it to look like someone has always lived there."

"Tracey can do that."

"Have her call me if she needs any more information, or if she runs out of budget. I gotta run." He hung up.

The computer on Stone's desk popped on with some information about streaming. After a moment, Joan came back into the room, elbowed Stone out of the way, and took over his keyboard. She tapped a few keys, then a few more, then an image popped onto the screen. Stone found himself looking at a large room with a group of people sitting around a conference table. The view was from high up in a corner of the room. Someone was operating the camera, because the picture zoomed slowly out, until nearly the whole space was on camera. The image was sharp and clear.

"Now, if you will excuse us," a man at the center of the table said, "we will retire to consider our decision." Everyone stood as they left the room and Stone now saw the Stone twins, dressed in suits and ties. Then the oddest thing happened: the two young men turned and stared up at the camera.

Stone had the immediate feeling that they were watching him. They were apparently not wearing microphones, but there was a live mic somewhere in the room which caught a murmur of what they were saying. Stone was certain that the name "Barrington" came from the lips of one of them. A chill ran through him.

Stone got up from his desk and sat on the sofa. "Let me know when something else happens," he said to Joan.

"I take it that those are the twins," she said from Stone's chair.

"Clever of you to figure that out," Stone said, "since they're identical."

"You don't want to watch this?"

"Looking at them makes me a little sick to my stomach," Stone replied. "Besides, nothing is happening. They're just staring at the camera." He stretched out on the sofa. "I'm going to take a nap."

"Suit yourself."

Stone closed his eyes and took a few deep breaths, then drifted off.

Then Joan was calling him. "Wake up! The jury is back!"

Stone sat up and rubbed his eyes. "They're not a jury; they're a parole board."

"Same thing," she said, rising from his chair.

Stone moved to his desk. The board's chairman was rapping on the table with a gavel. "The board has made a decision," he said. "By a vote of five to two, parole of Eben and Enos Stone is granted. Terms and conditions will be discussed by the parolees with their new parole officer. Before we adjourn, however, the governor's chief of staff, Edwin Ealy, would like to read to you a communication from the governor."

A man at the end of the table sat while the microphone was moved in front of him. "Go ahead, Mr. Ealy," the now-distant voice of the chairman said.

Ealy opened a leather envelope, removed a sheet of paper, and began to read:

I, Preston Farmer, the duly chosen governor of the State of Maine, do hereby pardon the defendants Enos Stone and Eben Stone of any and all crimes committed in the State of Maine up until this date, and I commute their sentences to time served.

Ealy distributed copies of the decree to the board members and to the Stone twins. "Gentlemen," he said, "you are free to go."

The chairman gaveled the meeting to a close, then a remarkable thing happened: the members of the parole board and the governor's chief of staff lined up to shake the twins' hands. Two of the three women on the board actually hugged and kissed them.

"Joan," Stone said, "please give me a couple of those Alka-Seltzer gummies you're so fond of." He sat and watched the people file out of the room, many of them stopping to shake the twins' hands. An attractive young blonde came and stood between them while somebody with a cell phone took their pictures, then the screen went dark.

"The feature has ended," Joan said. "Popcorn, Milk Duds, and Alka-Seltzer gummies on the concession stand to your right. The newsreel, cartoon, and adverts begin in one minute."

Stone chewed and swallowed his gummies, then lay back on the sofa and dropped off.

9

Stone had a sandwich at his desk and was refreshed by his nap. Joan buzzed him. "A Tracey Hotchkiss for you on one."

Stone picked it up. "Hello, Tracey."

"Hi, Stone. Billy tells me you're desperate for a decorator."

"No, just in a hurry."

"How fast do you want this done?"

"Last Thursday."

"Could you stand it if I took a month?"

"That would please me."

"If you'll authorize a trip to New York I can pick up showroom furniture samples and floor displays, have them delivered to a warehouse, then trucked up here toward the end of the project. We won't have to wait four months for special orders."

"I like it."

"In the meantime, I can get the painting and wallpapering and curtains done and be ready to place the furniture when it arrives."

"You're my kind of designer, Tracey."

"I used to do plays on Broadway and off, and the occasional movie. I learned how to do fast and good. I had a look at your house. Did you know that I designed it for Dick?"

"No, I didn't, but you did it right. By the way, I'll need a gun safe in a closet. And landscaping and flowers. Can you handle that?"

"With pleasure. I'll start moving earth tomorrow. Would you like paving on the driveway, or do you want to stick with dirt?"

"I think I'd like cobblestones from good Maine granite—on the walkways, too, but not too rough; I like smooth stones."

"Got it. We've just added about $150,000 to your budget."

"That's okay. You want a deposit?"

"I can use cash for buying a lot of your things. My fee is ten percent of everything, but I'll get you good enough prices to more than offset that."

"Great. I'll send cash today. I'll put you on with Joan for wiring details." He put her on hold and called Joan. "Wire this lady $250,000 on account, please, and tell her to let me know when she needs anything else."

They hung up, and Stone was happy for the first time that day.

Joan came into his office. "I sent her the quarter mil," she said. "Mind if I ask a question?"

"Shoot."

"Why are you buying and decorating and landscaping a house in a place where you already have a gorgeous home. Is this just to keep the twins from getting it?"

"Yes," Stone said. "There are other reasons, too, I think, but I don't know what they are."

Late that afternoon, Tracey called back. "I had a look around your new property this afternoon, and there's a barn building full of whatever was in the house before all the trouble. There are some glorious eighteenth-century American pieces of furniture, out of Boston and Newport— a dining table and chairs, a breakfront, and some other chests of drawers and odd tables. There's also a lot of old silver. They'll give the house great character."

"Then use them, but I don't want any upholstered furniture or bedding used. See that all of that is burned, in a responsible way, of course."

"Got it. I'll send you photographs as I progress."

"Don't. Surprise me when it's all done."

"As you wish." She hung up.

Later, after some thought, he called Tracey back. "I'd like you to put the eighteenth-century furniture and silver in my current house, and put the stuff it replaces into the new place."

"Good idea."

"One other thing about the new place: should the Stone twins ever chance to see it, I don't want them to recognize anything that used to belong to their side of the family."

"All right. By the way, Stone, Billy wants to talk to you."

"Put him on."

"Hey, Stone."

"Hey, Billy."

"A few minutes ago I got a call from a Boston lawyer named Keegan—the elder, not the younger. He represented the twins during negotiations for their sentencing, and his firm handled the details of their grandmother's estate."

"I know the Keegan son, but not the father."

"Well, apparently he's still representing them. They want to buy the family house."

"What did you tell him?"

"That it's been bought three times and sold twice. I stuck to the story we talked about—the Savannah lawyer and the Delaware corporation."

"You did the right thing, Billy."

"Keegan pressed me hard, but I told him it was out of my

hands. He said that the twins would be very, very disappointed to hear that. It sounded like a threat. I gave him the mailing address of the Delaware corporation, so you may be hearing from him."

"Good. I'll see that someone responds to it."

"Better you than me. Tracey is very excited about doing up the house."

"I'm delighted to have her do it," Stone replied. They said goodbye and hung up.

Stone knew he should start preparing to deal with the Stone twins, but he wasn't sure how, or what he would be dealing with. He hoped they kept it at the lawyer level, but he didn't believe that would happen.

He decided to deal with it on a blow-by-blow basis.

10

The Bacchettis returned to the city, and Stone and Dino arranged to have dinner at P. J. Clarke's. Viv was still dealing with jet lag after Hong Kong and L.A.

It was nearly seven, and they managed seats at the bar for drinks.

"So, how was your stay at the Arrington?"

"Flawless."

"And how are the boys?"

"Thriving. They're the toast of Hollywood, though they don't seem to know it."

"They're like that."

"Have you heard from the Stone twins yet?"

"You mean, 'heard' like a bomb through the window?"

"Something like that."

"So far, they're dealing through an attorney, Keegan."

"The one who came to see you?"

"His father. He's been representing them from the beginning of all this. He called Billy Hotchkiss, wanting to buy the house. Billy told him it was sold, and Keegan let it be known that the boys would be . . . 'very very disappointed,' if the sale closed."

"Has it closed?"

"Friday morning. I think Billy took some pleasure in telling him that. Also, I've hired his wife, Tracey, to decorate the place. She did Dick's house."

"Good. I can't see you running around town looking at swatches and paint chips."

"Good guess. She says she can have it done in a month."

"That's what they all say."

"She has movie and Broadway decorating experience. I believe her."

"The twins are going to make a move on you at some point," Dino said. "Are you ready for that?"

"No. All I can do is respond."

"My best guess is that they'll go for the house first."

Stone sat up straight. "I hadn't thought they'd do that."

"I'd call my insurance agent, if I were you."

"Not only that. I'm going to put some security on it."

"On Billy and Tracey, too."

"I'm not thinking fast at all. I'm glad you're back."

Stone sent his friend Mike Freeman, at Strategic Services, a text ordering help. "There, that'll get him started."

His phone rang. "Yes?"

"It's Mike. Is this about those twins?"

"It is."

"Oh, shit. I don't like what I'm hearing about that."

"It strikes me that an awful lot of people are hearing an awful lot of things about it. Tell your people to dress like residents, just arrived for the summer."

"What, did you think I would dress them like Secret Service, complete with palm mics?"

"Send some women, too. Give them station wagons, golf clubs, and tennis rackets."

"They'll like that. I'll have people there tomorrow morning."

"Thanks, Mike." He hung up.

"Listen, Stone," Dino said, "maybe these boys learned something in prison besides how to be better murderers. Maybe they're more normal now. A lot of people are saying that about them."

"You have a point, Dino, but I can't let myself think that way. You know, the first time I saw those boys was at the Taratine Yacht Club, on the island. What struck me was they were like fresh copies of their father at that age."

"Is the father the one you coldcocked when you were eighteen and got banished for your trouble?"

"One and the same. He was a shit then, and he was a shit until the day the boys put a gun to his head and blew his brains out. He seemed normal much of the time, but he wasn't normal, and I'm betting the twins aren't, either. Well, I'm not buying their act. I'm going to treat them as mortal threats."

"I'm sure those sentiments are returned in kind," Dino said.

"Me, too."

"You remember when we used to wear light armor to work?"

"Yes. It was hell in the summer."

"Not in Maine. It should be quite comfortable there."

Stone looked at him sharply. "Are you saying you think I'm going up there for the summer?"

"I'd say it's a sure thing, Stone. I know you well enough to think that you'll give the appearance of taking all this in stride, until you won't take it anymore. And my money would be on you, except . . ."

"Except what, Dino?"

"Except there are two of them."

"Well, everybody keeps telling me that they act as one man, that they're joined at the hip. If that's true, they'll make easier targets."

"With twice as much firepower. I'll help, but the mayor would frown on my spending the summer in Maine."

"Why don't you just retire, so you can be of more use to me?"

"Because I'd be busier than I am on the job," Dino said, laughing, "and in greater danger of bodily harm, too."

"Always thinking of yourself," Stone said.

"And my widow. Potentially."

"She'll be a rich and beautiful widow, and she'll draw men like flies."

"I know. Thanks for reminding me."

"Somebody's got to keep your head on straight."

"I'd just like to keep it attached," Dino said.

"I prefer it that way, too," Stone replied.

Dino was quiet for a moment. "Maybe the mayor will give me some unpaid leave—a month, say."

"I'll pay your salary."

"Will you stop reminding me that you're richer than I am?"

"Why? It's such fun."

"I'm rich enough to buy anything I want, if I'm careful about what I want."

"You're so wise, Dino. You should have been an owl."

"Maybe I can get Viv to volunteer," Dino said. "She's fond of you."

"I think she likes me better than you," Stone said.

"Yeah? If that's true, you've got more than the twins to worry about."

"With the two of you on the job, I'd have no worries. I could even take naps."

11

Stone had just finished with a client the following morning, when Joan buzzed. "Billy Hotchkiss on one for you."

Stone picked up the phone. "Hey, Billy."

"Hey, Stone. I got a call this morning you ought to know about."

"Uh-oh."

"Eben Stone was on the line. He says he and his brother are coming up here today to house hunt."

"'House hunt'?"

"You sound surprised."

"I thought they just wanted their old family place back."

"Apparently they've decided they want something bigger."

"Do you have anything like that on the books?"

"We've always got two or three white elephants—you

know, lots of rooms, but no insulation, leaky roofs, faulty appliances."

"Is that what they specified?"

"Not exactly, but it's all I've got this time of year. Season starts this weekend, so everything worth having sold in the spring."

"What are you going to do?"

"I'm going to show 'em houses, pal. It's what I do."

"Do you think you can horrify them out of wanting a summer there?"

"I'm going to give it my best shot. I'd sure like it if you were up here to watch my back."

"Billy, I've already sent people up there to do just that. Have you noticed a couple of folks moseying around your shop, not buying anything?"

"Now that you mention it. I've got one sitting on the porch, reading the *Boston Globe*. And another is looking at comic books and drinking our free water."

"That sounds like them. They'll be wearing loose-fitting garments to hide their weapons."

"I hope somebody's watching Tracey. She's down at the Stone place with half a dozen people, doing stuff. Hey, there went a truckload of granite paving stones just now."

"She's covered. Does the place have a security system?"

"Ah, no."

"I'll see to that. Get back to me if there's trouble, and I want a report on the twins."

"Okay."

Stone hung up, called Mike Freeman and asked him to get a security system into the house, pronto.

"The gear is already on a truck, due late this afternoon," Mike replied.

"You just keep staying ahead of me, Mike. I like that."

"I figured you'd want the deluxe package—cameras you can check on your iPhone, like that."

"Sounds good."

"In fact, if somebody rings the doorbell or comes to the gate, your phone will ring, and you can see who it is and tell 'em to go to hell."

"There's another piece of gear I need, Mike—two pieces, in fact."

"What's that?"

"I want a couple in late middle age, rich, retired-looking. They will be living there for a while, pretending to be the new owners."

"What are they retired from?"

"I don't care. They can make it up as they go along."

"Let me do some checking. I'm sure I can find a couple who'd enjoy a free summer in Maine. I'll call you back." Mike hung up.

Stone called Billy.

"Yeah, Stone?"

"I'm digging up a couple to pretend to be the new owners of the house," he said.

"That's good news. Do they exist?"

"They will, soon. They're going to be spending the summer in their new home. You'd better let Tracey know her clients will be there pretty soon."

"How soon?"

"I'll have to let you know."

"She's got a truckload of stuff arriving from New York the day after tomorrow," Billy said. "And they're working like beavers on the landscaping."

"Don't let the Stone boys see the place. It's not visible from the road, so it shouldn't be too difficult to keep them away from it."

"I'll put a sign out front."

"Saying what?"

"New owners arriving soon, but not yet."

"That ought to help."

"You tell them they won't need to bring a goddamned thing, except their clothes and toothbrushes. Tracey'll have it crammed full of everything else."

"I'll pass it on." Stone hung up.

Late in the afternoon, Stone's secure cell phone rang.

"Yes, Lance?"

"Good afternoon, Stone. I had a call earlier today from your friend Mike Freeman with a personnel problem—or perhaps, better, a casting problem."

"Yes."

"Right. I have a very fine married couple, who would look good in those roles, and they're retiring from our shop next month."

"I need them tomorrow."

"Well, then we'll give them a little terminal leave."

"Tell me about them."

"This is what the twins will learn if they're good with computers: Henry Lee and Grace Fowler Jackson. He is sixty-five, born in Thomasville, Georgia; she is sixty-one, born in Valdosta. Henry Lee, as he likes to be called, inherited a family machine-making business in Savannah a few years ago and he sold it three months ago. As a result, he has a net worth in the hundred-million-dollar bracket. They are fit, charming, friendly, and crack shots. The yacht and golf clubs will love them. They have a Dun & Bradstreet history, a sterling credit record, and a swollen stock portfolio. And they are graduates, three years apart, of the University of Georgia, in Athens, where they met. He also has an MBA from Georgia Tech where we recruited them right after Henry Lee's graduation. They've served in Britain, France, Germany and survived Lebanon. Sound interesting?"

"They sound perfect. How did you come up with all that so fast?"

"It helped a lot that they are real people, and what I read you is their real background."

"How much to rent them?"

"They don't rent out. I think they'll be happy with a free, comfortably furnished house."

"Do they know what they might be up against?"

"They're being briefed as we speak and reading up on the twins. When they're done, I'll put the offer to them. Will they have any special duties?"

"Just to live normal lives and not get killed."

"I'll get back to you, probably tomorrow." Lance hung up.

Stone began to feel better about the summer ahead.

12

Stone called Dino.

"Bacchetti."

"It's Stone. How soon can you start your extended leave?"

"What time is it now?"

"Ten-fifty-one."

"Give me until five o'clock to get my desk cleared and distribute some work I should be doing myself."

"That fast?"

"You need faster? I'll work on it."

"What got you so motivated?"

"Have you seen the weather forecast?"

"No."

"It's going to be ninety-five in the shade in New York tomorrow. There'll be a high of seventy-three in Bar Harbor."

"Say no more. Pick me up at eight AM; wheels up at nine-thirty."

"Viv's coming, too."

"Great, tell her I'm working on a new best friend for her."

"What about me?"

"You, too."

"I mean, besides you."

"Besides me."

"Tell me about them."

"I'm going to let you find out about them the same way everybody else does."

"Who are you bringing?"

"Nobody."

"That won't last long."

"From your lips to God's ear."

"See you tomorrow."

Stone hung up and buzzed Joan. "We're winging our way north to Maine tomorrow. Wheels up at nine-thirty; tell Faith to get it together."

"How long will you be there?"

"Remains to be seen."

"Can I come?"

"Are you kidding?"

"Yes."

"Good. Somebody's got to keep this ship afloat."

Their flight in Stone's Gulfstream 500 departed on time, with Stone at the controls. An hour later they landed in

Rockland, Maine, and taxied to the ramp, where Stone's Cessna 182 awaited. Luggage was shifted, and Stone turned over the G-500 to his pro pilot, Faith, and her hired copilot for the return trip to Teterboro. The short flight to Islesboro took less than fifteen minutes. As they turned final, for the runway, Stone glanced at the inbound ferry and saw a two-car flatbed truck was along for the ride from Lincolnville to Islesboro, carrying a station wagon and a convertible.

They landed and parked on the ramp there. Seth Hotchkiss, Stone's caretaker, awaited in the household's 1938 Ford woodie station wagon. Ten minutes later, they were home.

Stone's house had a family history, and a sad one. His first cousin Dick Stone and his wife and daughter were murdered there and the crime had been staged to make it look like a murder/suicide. Stone had inherited a lifetime occupancy of Dick's house, which had been bequeathed to a charity that assisted widows and orphans of CIA officers. Stone subsequently bought the property from the charity. Dick had been promoted to deputy director for operations, or DDO, but never had the opportunity to take office.

The house was a bulwark of personal safety. Built from CIA plans, it was sheathed in steel plating, rather than plywood, then the traditional cedar shingles over that. Still, the Stone family's murderers had managed entry. Stone knew in his bones that the twin sons of Dick's brother, Caleb, had committed the deed, though he couldn't prove it conclusively. The twins later confessed, when caught, of murdering Caleb and his wife, their parents.

They had some lunch, then Stone got up from the table. "I want to go over to the Dark Harbor Shop, get the *New York Times*, and have a word with Billy Hotchkiss."

"I'll come along," Dino said.

"I'll have a nap," Viv said.

Stone and Dino drove over in the little 1954 MG TF 1500 that had been restored by Dick. Billy was at his desk, as usual. "Welcome back," he said. "You, too, Dino."

The two men each pulled up a stool. "How much do you know?" Stone asked.

Billy lowered his voice; a customer or two wandered the shop. "I know that the folks from down south are called Henry Lee and Grace Jackson, and that they're arriving tomorrow afternoon in their own airplane."

"What kind of airplane?"

Billy consulted his notepad. "A Pilatus, a Swiss single-engine turboprop."

"Plenty of runway for that. How's Tracey coming along with the house?"

"I think you know she has a truckload of furniture

arriving from New York tomorrow at midday. By then, everything in the house will be in its place, ready to take the furniture. The Jacksons' two cars were shipped up here and arrived on the ferry half an hour ago—a Mercedes E450 station wagon and an S550 convertible, both with Georgia plates. The convertible is being unloaded at the house, now. The station wagon was left at the airport for their arrival."

Billy pointed at a passing flatbed truck. "There goes the delivery vehicle, back to the ferry."

"All very neat," Stone said.

"That's Tracey. She's a good manager."

"Have you heard anything of the boys or Keegan?"

"The twins arrived yesterday and checked into the inn. I showed them three houses: I think they're going to buy the best of them, down near the point, for a million and a half, or so. They'll need to spend another half million, or more, making it comfortable, with their grandmother's money. They've already talked to Hal Rhinehart about a new kitchen. He finished your house only last week, so he's available." Rhinehart was the island's resident cabinet-maker, as his father had been before him.

"Well," Stone said, "that should be good for the island's economy."

"I hope you're right," Billy said.

"Has there been any curiosity about the Jacksons?"

"The twins had a few questions. I gave them the party

line, in bits and pieces. By the middle of next week, everybody on the island will know everything there is to know about them."

Stone laughed. "With a little help from you."

"I do what I can," Billy said.

13

Stone and Dino got back in the MG. "Let's go see Ed Rawls," Stone said.

"And get shot for our trouble?"

Stone pulled over, stopped, and phoned Rawls.

"Speak."

"It's Stone. Dino and I are on the island, headed your way, with news."

"I'll buy you a drink, if you know something I don't know," Rawls said, then hung up.

The giant log that was Rawls's outer gate rolled away as they approached, then closed behind them. The inner gate, down by the house, opened, too. The view was of Penobscot Bay, and Rawls had a sturdy dock and boathouse, too.

Ed emerged as they pulled up to the porch. "Friend or foe?" he shouted.

"That depends on how good the booze is," Dino shouted back.

They were escorted into the living room, where Sally, an Englishwoman of Stone's acquaintance who had become Ed's live-in companion, was already pouring drinks.

Ed showed them to comfortable chairs. "Tell me something I don't know," he said to them.

"The Stone twins arrived on the island yesterday, house hunting. Looks like they're going to buy that old place down on the point."

Ed smote his forehead. "Sally, double up on those drinks." He sat down, while Sally poured. "How did you know that before I did?"

"I got to Billy Hotchkiss first."

"And I thought he was saving those tidbits for me."

"That's what everybody on the island thinks," Stone replied.

"I think they're up to no good," Ed said.

"Everybody knows that, too, we just don't know what."

"Should I just kill them now and save us all the anxiety?"

"That's an outstanding idea," Stone said, "but I don't think it's going to be that easy."

"Yeah, I heard about all that boxing and Japanese sticks and all. You think they got smarter, too?"

"I think they were always smart."

"Lance says . . ." Rawls paused. He was retired CIA. Once he had had a little band of Agency retirees up here, who called themselves "the Old Farts." Ed was the last of them.

"I'd *really* like to know what Lance says today," Stone said. "I know what he thought yesterday."

"He says we're going to have to wait for them to make the first move."

"No hurrying things along, huh?"

"That's about the size of it."

"How do we provoke them?" Stone asked.

"Walk around without a weapon," Rawls said.

"You think?"

"That ought to do it. Or find some other way to look vulnerable."

"Without actually being vulnerable, you mean?"

"Preferably."

"How do you do that?"

"I haven't figured it out yet."

"You know about Henry Lee and Grace?"

"The Jacksons? I knew them thirty years ago. They were the golden kids of operations. What about them?"

"Jesus, Ed, you're not keeping up."

"Enlighten me."

"You know I bought the Stone house out from under the twins?"

"That, I know."

"Using a Delaware corporation for cover?"

"Yep."

"Well, Billy is putting the word out that Henry Lee and Grace are the board of directors and only stockholders. They're arriving tomorrow to take possession, and Tracey is making miracles over there as we speak."

"Do they know about the Stone twins' interest in the place?"

"They do, and they're coming armed."

"I would expect no less of them. Do you think the twins will go after them?"

"It's been thought that they might. If they don't make a move, we will let it be known that I'm the guy behind the Jacksons."

"Well, if the scent of your blood isn't enough to move the boys off square one, I don't know what is," Rawls said.

"One thing we have on our side is that the twins have a lot more to lose than they used to. In fact, they seem to have just about everything they want in the world, except that house."

"Have they got a boat?" Rawls asked.

"I don't know. Why do you ask?"

"A boating accident is always good."

"Let's hope they get a boat," Stone said.

"Let's hope they get a gasoline-powered one. I mean, if you're looking for a tragic accident to happen, gasoline is always a good place to start."

"Your view is so reasonable, it's hard to argue with it," Stone said.

"If you're in the mood to employ gasoline, why not just commit a little arson on their house, as soon as they buy it?" Rawls asked.

"Because renovating it will keep them busy for a while. When it's all done and ready to move into, then's the time to torch it."

"Not after they move in and are fast asleep?"

"That's an inviting thought."

Dino broke in. "You forget that these kids have stayed alive and well in prison for several years. They must be good at it."

"I can tell you from experience," said Rawls, who had done some time in his past, "that one gains wariness as a normal state of mind."

"And they can take turns sleeping," Dino pointed out.

"This is a problem we don't have to solve before we finish this drink," Stone said.

"You have a point," Rawls agreed.

"Since we're in a murderous mood," Stone said, "why don't we just let the idea roll around our occipital lobes. After it's simmered there for a while, it might just, willy-nilly, develop into a plan that we could act on."

"The best thing about your plan," Dino said, "is that we don't have to do anything until later." He tossed off the remainder of his drink, and Sally approached with the Scotch.

"Just leave the bottle, darlin'," Rawls said, reaching for it.

14

Stone and Dino got into the MG, negotiated the two security gates, and headed toward home.

"It occurs to me," Dino said, "that we haven't found an interesting woman for you."

"Oh, stop it."

"Why don't we pop into the shop for an ice cream cone? That should do it. Pull over."

"The ice cream part of that sounds good," Stone said, turning into a parking space. They got out and walked up the steps to the porch. Stone could not help but notice that a tallish blonde in tweedy clothes sat, stretched out in a rocker, absorbed in licking a cone with her left hand, which gave Stone the opportunity to spot the bare third finger. He stopped. "That looks like a very interesting ice cream cone," he said. "What is the flavor?"

"Bourbon praline," she replied and returned to licking it.

Stone went into the shop and ordered a two-scooper, while Dino perused the *Times*, then he walked back outside. "May I join you?" Stone asked, indicating the rocker conveniently empty beside her.

"Please, do," she slurped.

"I took your advice," Stone said, contemplating his cone.

"It wasn't advice, just information," she replied.

Stone tried it. "If it had been advice," he said, "it would have been very good."

"I'm happy for you."

"Usually," he said, "when I enjoy bourbon, I take it directly from the source."

"The barrel?"

"Just the bottle. Sometimes with a straw."

Dino came out of the shop, the paper tucked under his arm. "Are you ready?" he asked Stone.

"I'm just getting started," Stone replied. "Go get yourself some bourbon praline. She recommends it." He nodded at the woman.

"How can I resist?" Dino asked, disappearing into the shop.

"That was my friend, Dino," he said to the woman.

"Is he an interesting person?"

"Usually."

"He appears to be from south of here."

"Way south," Stone said. "He's the police commissioner of New York City."

"That *is* interesting."

"I try to travel with a bodyguard."

"Do others seek your demise?" she drawled. Her accent was Brahmin New England, and broad.

"From time to time. Dino must not suspect you, since he has left us alone."

"He may have misjudged me," she said.

"I hope not. My name is Stone Barrington." He offered her a hand, and she shook it with long fingers.

"I am Hester Primrose."

Stone suppressed a laugh. "Really?"

"Really. But you may call me Primmy. Everyone I like does."

"What do those you don't like call you?"

"Hester. Can you imagine?"

"I cannot. Primmy, if I may be so bold, are you a free woman?"

She turned and looked at him directly for the first time with bright blue eyes, to go with the blond ponytail. "In every sense of the word," she replied.

"Oh, good. We—Dino and his wife, Vivian, and I—are dining at my house around seven. We would be very pleased if you would join us. I live at . . ."

"I know where you live," she said.

"Shall we say six-thirty, for drinks?"

"Perfect."

"We will not dress up for dinner."

"Excellent. I'm not sure I even own a dress anymore."

"You're perfect as you are."

"Something every woman loves to be told. You're not bad yourself, you know."

Dino reappeared with an ice cream cone. "Ready?"

"Primmy, may I present my friend Dino Bacchetti? Dino, this is Hester Primrose, who prefers to be called Primmy."

"Who could blame her?" Dino asked, shaking her hand. "How do you do?"

"I do very nicely, thank you," Primmy replied.

"Do you want to finish your cone before we depart?" Stone asked Dino.

"Why bother? You're driving."

"Quite right," Stone replied, wolfing down what was left of his cone. "See you at six-thirty, Primmy."

"You may count on it."

They got into the car. Stone got it started, then headed for home.

"The time it took to buy an ice cream cone seems to have been enough," Dino said.

"I got lucky."

"You usually do."

As they turned off at Stone's driveway, an elderly Mercedes convertible, top down, passed them going the other way.

"What was that?" Stone asked. "A fifty-seven 300?"

"More or less," Dino said. "Did you see who was driving?"

"No," Stone replied. "I was absorbed with the car—a very nice specimen. They must have just got off the ferry."

"Probably."

"I've always liked that year for Mercedes," Stone said.

"Why, did you used to drive one?"

"No, at the time I became able to recognize the model, I couldn't yet afford one."

"Why don't you buy one now?"

"My garages, both here and in New York, are too crowded," Stone replied.

"You didn't recognize the driver, then?"

"No. Was it the Jacksons?"

"I've never seen the Jacksons, but I'm certain it was not."

"Why?"

"It was being driven by one of the Stone twins," Dino said. "Take your pick."

15

They had finished lunch and had divided up the *Times*, when the phone rang. Stone had a sudden twinge and hoped that Ms. Primrose was not calling to cancel. "Hello?"

"It's Billy. The twins bought the house, the one down near the point. Get this: they've already engaged a builder from Camden for the renovation. He's going to bring his crew over on the seven AM ferry every day and they will depart on the four o'clock."

"Have they already closed?"

"Monday morning," Billy said. "They're faster than even you. They tried to hire Tracey, too, but she declined as gracefully as she could."

"Smart girl."

"I hope she was graceful enough."

"So do I," Stone said.

"Something else. They asked me about cleaning their family stuff out of the barn at the old house."

"What did you reply to that?"

"I explained that the contracts among the past two owners specified that the contents of all buildings were included in the sale."

"How did they take that?"

"Not well. They said they'd make the new owner an offer."

"One that he can't refuse?"

"Let's not go there."

"Have the Jacksons arrived yet?"

"They phoned from the air: ETA is two PM. I'm meeting them at the airstrip."

Stone glanced at his watch: half an hour. "It's important that I meet them before the twins do," he said. "Can you ask them to expect me to drop by around three-thirty?"

"All right."

"Thank you, Billy." He hung up.

"Was that Billy?"

"It was, and with bad news."

"They already bought the house?"

"You guessed it."

"And you're meeting the Jacksons at three-thirty?"

"You're a good listener, Dino. I thought I'd invite them for dinner tonight. It's a chance to get to know them, and it'll give Primmy something to gossip about around the island."

Something fairly loud flew over at a low altitude. "I think that's the Jacksons' Pilatus landing now. They're a little early.

"Want me to go with you?" Dino asked.

"No, you'll meet them tonight anyway."

"As you wish," Dino said. He went into Dick Stone's little office and used the copying machine, then returned and gave both Stone and Viv copies of the *Times* crossword.

Stone worked on it until it was time to go meet the Jacksons.

He drove down in the MG. The gate was near Ed Rawls's entrance, and theirs had an entry pod set up by an inner gate. Stone pressed the buzzer and gazed into the camera.

"Yes?" A tinny voice.

"It's Stone Barrington."

The gate opened immediately, then closed behind him.

Both Jacksons met him at the door and introduced themselves. They were handsome people, Stone thought, appearing younger than their years.

"Have a seat," Henry Lee said.

"Do you mind if I have a look around first?" Stone asked.

"Sure. I'll go with you," Henry Lee replied. "I haven't seen it all myself, yet."

"I'll get us some lemonade," Grace said.

The two men walked through the house slowly, inspecting.

"It looks like the last people who lived here forgot to move out when they left," Henry Lee said. "And it's really nice furniture."

There was a living room, dining room, kitchen, and a paneled study on the ground floor, and four bedrooms and baths upstairs. The master suite had two baths and dressing rooms.

"The garage is off the kitchen," Henry Lee said.

They went back into the living room and sat down. Lemonade was served.

"I know you've been well briefed, but I just want to bring you up to date," Stone said.

"You mean about the twins buying a house?" Henry Lee asked.

"Oh, that's right. Billy met you at the airfield. He told you about the barn problem, then?"

"Yes, and we had a look at it. It's empty and clean as a whistle," Grace said.

"About the front gate," Stone said. "I'd leave it open in the daytime. The neighbors won't like to see it closed. Close it at bedtime."

"Duly noted," Grace said.

"Have you had a chance to familiarize yourselves with the security system?"

"It's the standard Agency equipment, with a few new flourishes," Henry Lee said. "We can actually see the property on-screen and peoples' faces when they're at the gate or door."

"Good. Use it. You brought arms?"

"We did."

"Keep them ready to use. Know that, if you feel it necessary to kill one or both of them, local law enforcement will look kindly on your actions. In fact, if you kill one of them, you'd better kill the other, too."

"Got it," Henry Lee said. "I appreciate you taking the time to talk to us."

"I'd like to invite the two of you to dinner at my house, this evening," Stone said.

"We'd be delighted," Grace said.

He gave them directions. "Six-thirty, for drinks. My friends from New York, Dino and Vivian Bacchetti, will be there . . ."

"We've been briefed on them, too."

"And a local woman, Hester Primrose, who prefers Primmy. I think we can count on her to spread the word about you among the summer residents."

"That's grand," Henry Lee said.

"I'd better get home, then," Stone said, rising. "I hope this turns out to be a vacation for you, rather than a chore."

"We're enjoying it already," Grace said. They walked him to the door.

"I must say, Tracey Hotchkiss did a wonderful job on the place."

"You mean, it wasn't always like this?" Henry Lee asked.

They waved him off.

16

They waited for Primmy to arrive before having their first drink. Her taste in clothing reminded Stone of Katharine Hepburn, a neighbor in Turtle Bay before her death, that is to say, eccentric. She wore suede pants with a Hermès scarf tied around her waist, like a skirt, and a tweed jacket. She was taller than Stone had imagined, pushing six feet, he estimated, and she filled out a sweater beautifully. She and Viv were introduced and got on immediately.

While Stone was mixing their drinks, the Jacksons arrived and introductions were reaccomplished.

"How did you come to be named Hester?" Grace asked Primmy. "Did your mother hate you?"

Primmy laughed. "No, she was very sweet. I was named after my grandmother's sister—who had somehow cornered most of the family money—in the hope that she would be good to me in her will. It worked. What do you two do, Grace?"

"I worked abroad for a family business, a machine-tooling company," Henry Lee said. "I set up offices in various foreign cities and looked for customers."

"I shopped," Grace said, "and ran whatever house or flat we were occupying. Once Henry Lee had established relationships in a region, we could move on to another, and he could maintain customer relations by phone and e-mail."

"Sounds like you two would have been perfect for the CIA," Primmy said.

Henry Lee didn't miss a beat. "You're not the first to have told us that."

Stone changed the subject. "Primmy, did your ancestors come over on the *Mayflower*?"

"No, but on the next boat, the following year."

"Did they bring the accent with them?" Grace asked.

"No, I think that just grew, like Topsy."

Stone turned to Grace. "Do you know about the history of your new house?"

"Some, I guess."

"I can give it to you in a nutshell," Stone said. "I spent a summer in that house when I was eighteen, with my first cousins, Dick and Caleb Stone."

"Which one fathered the twins?" Grace asked. Stone had sketched a brief history of those two for Primmy's benefit.

"Caleb. He and I didn't get along very well, but Dick and I were close. Caleb and I eventually came to blows. At least, I did. His mother banished me from the island forever after that."

Stone told them about the murders of Dick and his family, and about the twins and what they were suspected of. "Primmy," he said, "you should steer clear of the twins. They're buying the old house down near the point. Avoid meeting them, if possible."

Primmy gave a little shudder. "I certainly will," she said.

"Perhaps they learned some manners in prison," Henry Lee ventured.

"I'm more likely to believe they did what all too many criminals do in prison," Stone said. "They become better criminals."

They were called to dinner and treated to Mary's lobster pie, and a couple of bottles of a fine chardonnay from Dick Stone's cellar.

Shortly after they were on cognac, Stone's phone rang.

"Yes?"

"It's Rawls. Somebody's messing around my new neighbors' place."

"Shall I join you?"

"Please do."

Stone hung up. "Henry Lee, one of your neighbors, Ed

Rawls, says someone is paying too much attention to your property. Want to join me in having a look?"

"Sure. Grace, you keep the others company, please."

Grace nodded.

Stone took the old Ford station wagon.

"They're not wasting any time, are they?" Henry Lee said.

"Nope, and that's disturbing."

They were met by Rawls at the Jacksons' gate. "Hey, Henry Lee." He and Jackson shook hands warmly. "How you been?"

"Slogging toward the pension," Henry Lee replied. "Nearly there." He opened the gate with his iPhone.

"Let's not split up," Stone said. "If they're here, I'd like us to outnumber them."

The three men walked abreast toward the house.

"Let's start with the barn," Stone said, "since they've expressed an interest in that. Can you turn off the alarm, Henry Lee?"

"Sure." He did so.

Rawls produced a small but powerful flashlight and played it over the barn doors as they approached. Once there, he played it over the hardware on the door. "A few scratches that look recent," he said. "What's in here?"

"Absolutely nothing," Henry Lee replied.

"Tracey Hotchkiss cleaned up what was useful and got rid of the rest," Stone said. "Billy says the boys wanted the contents, and I expect they're pissed off about it."

"Pissed off is not the state of mind I'd want them in," Rawls said.

"What would you prefer?" Henry Lee asked.

"Fat, dumb, and happy."

"I'm afraid you're not going to get any of those wishes," Stone said.

"Let's check out the house," Henry Lee said. He let them in through the front door and they looked around. "Looks untouched," Stone said.

"Henry Lee," Rawls said. "Can you tell if the security system has been tampered with?"

Henry Lee went to a keypad. "I can reset it, and it will give me messages." He watched the screens flash by as tests were run.

"This is a new version, since I installed mine," Ed said.

"That's because you're old, Ed," Stone replied.

"I installed it last year."

"Oh."

The keypad made a chirping noise and displayed READY.

"One successful entry was made in our absence," Henry Lee said. "About twenty minutes ago."

"That's about when I saw a flash of light from over here," Rawls said.

"Let's hope this visit satisfied the twins' curiosity," Stone remarked.

They got back in the car and returned to their dinner party, which was waning. Their guests soon went home.

17

Stone asked Primmy to stay on for another cognac, and she did. "We hardly got to talk at all," he said.

"You're right," she replied. "Kindly explain your marital status to me."

"I'm a widower."

"Ahh."

"And you?"

"Divorced twice, one recently."

"I'm sorry, if you are," Stone said.

"Not in the least. I have a history of attracting men who have expensive tastes and little money, and I'm always glad to see them go."

"I don't blame you."

"Gentlemanly charm is a heady thing," she said, "but I've discovered it's more attractive when attached to an income."

"I expect so. If it matters, I have a policy of not pursuing women who have more money than I."

"May I ask you a personal question?"

"As long as you don't expect an honest answer."

She laughed. "Not *that* personal."

"Shoot."

"How much money do you have?"

"That's not only personal, but rude. You first."

"I believe that's called being hoisted on my own petard."

"If you're not willing to answer the question, why should I?"

"All right, after the most recent divorce, I'm left nearly penniless. About twenty million bucks. Now you."

"More than you," Stone replied.

"That's not fair!"

"Why not? It should allay your fears."

"Really now!"

"All right, a *lot* more than you."

"That's a little better. I suppose I'm going to have to work harder at this. How many houses do you have?"

"Let's see." Stone counted on his fingers. "New York, here, Los Angeles, Paris, London, Beaulieu, in Hampshire. I'm out of fingers."

"Are there mortgages on any of them?"

"No."

"I'm feeling better now. Do you own an airplane?"

"Two."

"What sort?"

"A Gulfstream 500 and a small Cessna, kept here, for getting to and from Rockland Airport."

"Congratulations," she said, "you are fully qualified."

"For what?"

"To pursue my virtue, but not my fortune."

"Come closer," he said.

She hipped her way across the sofa and threw a leg over his. "Will that do?"

"It's a good start. You know, with the twins hovering about, I don't think you should go home alone in the dark."

"Then you'll drive me?"

"No. I have only two cars, and neither is suitable for repelling boarders."

"Then I'm afraid you'll have to offer me a bed."

"There's only one available, and it's already occupied."

"By whom?"

"By me."

"Will you share?"

"I will."

She kissed him long enough to arouse his interest. "Will you carry me upstairs?"

"Sorry, bad back."

"So, I'll have to carry you?"

"I can manage on my own, if you can."

"Let's find out," she said, grabbing her snifter and heading for the stairs.

Stone followed. "Turn right at the top. A left would cause embarrassment for everyone."

She turned right.

"Where's the bathroom?"

Stone switched on a small lamp. "Yours is there," he said, pointing.

"Be right back."

He lit the fire and got into bed.

"Ooh, a fire!" she said, striding toward him, naked.

"You look very nice by firelight," he said.

"Now, that's just the sort of thing a man should say to get a girl interested."

"You look very nice, *naked*, by firelight."

She climbed into bed and into his arms. "There," she said, with satisfaction.

It took a bit longer to satisfy Stone.

18

Ed Rawls was taking out his trash early the next morning when he heard what, to his ear, sounded like a column of armored vehicles approaching his gate, from the direction of the village. Instinctively, he took cover behind the structure that held his refuse cans, and to his surprise, the column turned out to be vehicles of the building trades. First was a dump truck, apparently empty, followed by a backhoe on a trailer, three large vans, emblazoned with the name of a Camden builder, then the vans of an electrician and a plumber, then a small bus, which seemed to hold about a dozen men. They passed by and disappeared down the road to the point. "Jesus, Mary, and Joseph," he said, when the noise had melted away.

———

After breakfast, he and Sally took his boat out and cruised slowly down the bay toward the southern tip of the island. Eventually, the old house came into view. It had the appearance of a beehive, crawling with worker bees. The roof looked good, he thought. Somebody had put a new one on three or four years ago, he remembered. He got out his binoculars and let the boat drift.

The dump truck was being filled with chunks of plaster, but he didn't see any stacks of drywall waiting, so, he reasoned, they must intend to replaster the interior. To confirm his notion, he saw a plasterer's truck pull up to the house, a little late to the party.

"Ed," Sally said, peering through her own binoculars, "if you were doing up this house, how would you go about it?"

"I think," he said, "just about the same way they're doing it, if I had the money. I'd rip out the old plaster, then set the plumber replumbing and the electrician rewiring. And when they finished, I'd replaster. The roof's okay, the floorboards are sturdy, I imagine."

"How long will they take?"

"How long a house takes is a function of how many warm bodies are working on it. If you've got five, it'll take forever. If you've got two dozen, things will move along quickly. They won't hold still long enough for me to count 'em."

"Is there anything sinister in the way they're doing it?"

"Expensive, yes. Sinister, no—unless you've got a house down in Camden that needs renovation, and you're trying to find the people to do it. Looks like the Stone boys have pretty much dried up the local labor pool. They seem to be building the same way Tracey Hotchkiss decorates interiors. At lunchtime folks'll be talking of nothing else over at the yacht club."

Stone was halfway through his morning when his cell phone rang.

"Good morning," Lance Cabot said. "I'm in the neighborhood. Could I camp out in your guesthouse for a few days?"

"Of course, Lance. You're always welcome."

"Oh, good. I have to drop off a housewarming gift for the Jacksons, then I'll be over in time for lunch."

"You're already on the island?"

"I am; you'll be interested in what came over on the same ferry as I." He hung up.

Dino and Viv came down the stairs. Primmy had yet to surface.

"Lance Cabot is joining us. He'll be staying in the guesthouse."

"When?" Dino asked.

"Any minute, I expect."

———

Lance walked in fifteen minutes later. "Hello, everybody; what's for lunch?"

"I thought we'd stroll over to the yacht club and have some of their famous burgers."

"Sounds good."

"What did you see on the ferry?" Stone asked.

"I was lucky to get aboard," Lance said. "It was filled with an army of construction people and their equipment, worthy of the Seabees. I followed them down the road toward the point as far as the Jacksons' place, where I left their gift on the front porch, then returned here."

"They had to be headed to the Stones' new house," Stone said. "Billy Hotchkiss told me they were starting today." Stone looked up to see Primmy descending the stairs, looking fresh and new.

"Ah, Primmy!" Lance shouted, gathering her up for a hug and a kiss at the bottom of the stairs. "I didn't know you knew Stone."

"I didn't, Lance, until recently." She seemed unabashed that she had been spotted leaving Stone's bedroom.

There was a little catching up to do. It seemed that Lance had known Primmy's family when he was at Harvard.

"Shall we adjourn to the yacht club?" Stone asked. "It's early, and we'll need a big table."

They strolled the fifty yards to the club and secured a table, just ahead of the rush. They were halfway through their lunch when the screen door slammed, and the room fell silent, just for a moment.

Stone turned to see who had elicited that response and saw, standing at the door, looking for a table, his two second cousins, Eben and Enos Stone. To his astonishment, they began making the rounds of the room, saying hello to anyone they knew.

They stopped at Stone's table; he met them with a glacial stare.

"Hello, Cousin Stone," they said in unison, as usual.

"Move on," Stone said. "And as far as I'm concerned, you can keep moving."

The twins went to the lunch counter, picked up an order they had apparently called in, then left, followed by a smattering of applause and some hisses.

The commodore of the club visited a few tables, asking questions. Finally, he stopped at Stone's party. "Need I ask what you feel about the Stone twins?" he asked.

"I feel that, if they are still on the club's rolls at sundown, I will resign," Stone replied. "I mean no offense to you. They have placed you in a difficult position. But I believe them to be the murderers of Dick Stone, his wife, and daughter, who were also members of this club."

"I understand perfectly," the man said. "I've already called a board meeting for three o'clock."

"If you need reinforcements," Stone said, "please let me know. I can be here in five minutes."

"From the reaction I've had so far, I won't need any help."

Stone led his party back to the house. At ten minutes past three o'clock his phone rang. "Yes?"

"It's Billy. I thought you'd like to know that the board of the yacht club voted unanimously to remove the Stone twins from the membership list. Their boat has been towed from the club's docks and left on a public mooring, in a disadvantageous spot."

Stone put down the phone. "The club's board is notifying the membership, by the fastest possible means, according to Billy Hotchkiss, that the twins are no longer members."

Followed by several versions of "Hooray."

19

L ance took a call and covered the phone. "It's Henry
Lee Jackson," he said. "He wants me to come to dinner there, but he warns it will be noisy, if the builders down
the road work late." He held the phone away from his ear,
and a loud noise erupted from it. A moment later, they
heard a boom from outside. "Apparently, they're shifting
some ledge down there."

"Invite the Jacksons here," Stone said.

Lance did so.

Primmy spoke up, "The noise is going to affect my property, too. I'm closer to the twins than the Jacksons."

Stone took her aside. "I think you should move in with
me, until this business with the twins has been resolved."

"Sold," she said. "I'd better go pack a bag before it gets
dark."

"Primmy, are you licensed to carry a gun in Maine?"

"I am."

"Then come armed, and don't linger down at that end of the island. Shall I come with you?"

"Of course not. I'll be back in an hour." She left the house.

Stone went back to the others. "Primmy has gone to pack. She's moving in here for the duration, and she's coming armed. I suggest that you all carry while you're here." He went to tell Mary how many they would be for dinner.

Primmy drove slowly past the Stones' house, to satisfy her curiosity about what was going on there. "The place is an anthill," she said aloud to herself. She drove on to her place, two driveways down. She pulled into the yard and went inside. She, like pretty much everyone else on the island, didn't bother locking her doors. She went upstairs to her bedroom, got down two suitcases and began stuffing things into them. She closed the larger one, wheeled it to the stairs, and started rolling it down. A deep voice made her jump and lose control of the case, which bounced into the living room and stopped.

"Can we give you a hand?"

She stopped and looked at them. She wasn't sure which one had spoken. "I can manage, thank you."

One of them picked up the bag as if it were a briefcase.

"I'll put it in your trunk," he said, then turned and walked out the door.

Primmy, her heart pounding, ran back up the stairs, opened the safe in her dressing room and took out a compact 9mm and its holster. She was fitting it onto her belt, her back to the door, when someone said, "Is this one ready to go?"

She pulled down her shirttail over the holster and turned to find a twin standing in her bedroom. "I don't believe I invited you into this room," she said. "In fact, I don't believe I invited you into my house. Please leave now."

A smile spread slowly across his face. "We don't always wait for invitations from beautiful women," he said. "They seem to prefer it that way."

"Apparently, your ego is larger than your brain," Primmy said. She was less nervous than angry now.

"I believe that was an insult," he said.

"Well, your hearing is working. I'm not going to tell you again to get out of my house." She reached under her shirt, thumbed off the snap from the holster, and kept her hand on the butt of the pistol.

"You scratching an itch under there?" he asked. "Maybe I can scratch it for you." He took a step toward her.

Primmy, in one smooth motion, pulled the pistol and racked the slide and pointed it at the floor.

"Well, now," he said. "That's not very hospitable—more hostile, I'd say."

"You want to see hostile?" she asked, raising the pistol

and thumbing off the safety. Her finger still rested along-side the trigger, not on it.

"Yeah," he said. "We enjoy a little hostility in a woman."

Primmy aimed over his shoulder at the doorjamb and squeezed off a round. The sound came in concert with another blast from the house down the road, and she was appalled to see his head jerk to one side and a little puff of blood erupt from his ear.

The twin clapped a hand over his ear and backed toward the stairs slowly. "I'm going to take pleasure in making you regret that," he said.

"Don't walk, run!" she shouted at him. He turned and started down the stairs, looking back at her over his shoulder. Beyond him, the other twin was starting up the stairs. She kicked the nearest one hard in the ass; he lost his footing and tumbled down the stairs on top of his brother, the two of them ending up in a heap.

She took a step on the stairs. "I'm sorry I missed," she said. "I'll try to do better this time." She fired another at the floor to one side of them. They were scrambling to get out of the house now.

She followed them down the stairs and to the door, her pistol held out in front of her. The two leapt into a pickup truck and reversed up the driveway, leaving a rosebush in distress.

Primmy slammed the door and ran upstairs, holstering the weapon. She went to the safe and got a box of ammunition and a spare magazine, tossed them into her suitcase with her underwear, grabbed the case, and pushed it down the stairs ahead of her. She let herself out, locked up the house, set the alarm system, tossed her bag into the trunk with the first, got into the car, and drove back to Stone's house, doing her best not to drive faster than the speed limit. She didn't want to have to explain all this to the single state trooper on the island.

Stone let her in. "You're all flushed," he said. "What happened?"

"I'll tell you when my bags are safe inside," she said, heading for the bar, everyone staring at her. By the time Stone got the cases upstairs she has halfway through a large Scotch, no ice.

"All right," Stone said, pouring her another. "Tell me what happened."

"I took a shot at a twin," she said. "I don't suppose it matters which one."

"Did you hit him?"

"Sort of. I was aiming past him, but I guess I was in a hurry or, maybe, he moved. I nicked his ear."

"How did he react to that?"

"He was displeased," she said. "His brother tried to help, but I fired another round to discourage them, and they got out. So did I, as fast as I could."

"Well done," Stone said, and the others gave her a round of applause.

20

They were just finishing their drinks before dinner when they heard the rumble of the construction caravan pass, apparently on its way to the ferry.

Stone glanced at his watch. "They put in a long day," he noted.

"I wonder why they didn't leave the equipment and just take the bus onto the ferry," Lance said.

"I'm not sure about this," Stone said, "but I think there may be a rule against leaving heavy equipment parked on the island overnight."

The doorbell rang and Stone answered it. Finding the Jacksons standing there, he ushered them in. "I think you know everybody here," he said. "Can I get you a drink?"

"Thanks, but we had one, sitting upstairs and watching

the construction people getting out in time for the ferry. It was precision stuff."

"We saw them moving a few pieces of furniture into the house, so I expect they've finished a bedroom enough to live in during construction," Henry Lee said.

"I'm sorry to hear that," Primmy said. "It means I can't go home again after dark."

"No need to go home at all," Stone said. "You're entirely welcome here."

"I don't think the twins will be on the island all the time," Lance said.

"What do you know that we don't know?" Stone asked.

"The boys are teaching a course two days a week at Yale Law, during summer school."

"What course?" Henry Lee asked.

"Criminal appeals. They apparently wrote over a hundred successful ones while in prison."

"The arcane nature of your knowledge never fails to amaze me, Lance," Stone said.

"So much is provided daily," Lance replied, "and I have a better memory than any human being needs. My brain sorts it, then retains anything that might be of any use, ever, and dumps the rest."

"You poor man," Viv said. "Dino can barely remember his phone number."

"I could always remember yours, though," Dino replied.

"A saving grace," Viv said, blowing him a kiss.

"What days do they teach?" Henry Lee asked.

"Tuesday and Wednesday, I believe."

"So we can all sleep safely in our beds tonight," Grace said. "But how do they get to New Haven?"

"They used to have an airplane," Stone said. "A Cessna 182, like mine. I shouldn't think they've had time to requalify, though."

"Perhaps Yale doesn't start summer school until next week," Lance ventured.

"Well, if they've kept current with their reading while in the joint, they could do the flying in a couple of days, I guess. It's a simple airplane."

"I don't much like the idea of their being able to travel so easily," Lance said.

"Neither do I," Stone said. "I wonder what they drive."

Primmy spoke up. "A pickup truck," she said. "Red and newish-looking. I know because it took out one of my rosebushes as they were leaving."

"They must have been in a hurry," Henry Lee said.

"I don't know why. I only fired on them twice."

That got a laugh.

"Billy said they have a boat, too, but I didn't ask what kind. In any case, it's been banned from the yacht club dock and moorings."

"It's a pity they couldn't be banned from the island," Lance said. "Is that possible?"

"I shouldn't think so," Stone replied. "It's usually enough if they can't get into the club. I don't think anybody who was blackballed has ever lasted more than a season."

"Well," Lance said, "they've already been kicked out of the club. That's a start."

"It didn't stop them from buying a house," Stone pointed out, "but it will certainly curtail their social lives. It's not as though there's a lot to do here, except for sailing, golf, and tennis."

"And what we're doing," Primmy said to Stone, nudging him.

"Well, there is that, isn't there?" Viv said, smirking.

A tiny, repetitive beep started.

"What's that sound?" Dino asked.

"It's from the security system," Stone said.

"What does it mean?"

"It's telling us that there's somebody on the property on foot." He rose. "Dino, shall we take a short stroll?"

"Why not?" Dino got up.

"Need help?" Henry Lee asked.

"Not unless you hear gunfire," Stone said. "We'll be right back."

21

Stone retrieved a couple of small flashlights from a drawer and tossed one to Dino. "Don't use that, unless you absolutely have to. It will just make you a target."

"Gotcha," Dino replied.

Stone switched off the back porch light. The two of them checked their weapons, then stepped outside. Stone held out a hand. "Listen. Hear anything?"

They both listened. Branches were snapping and leaves rustling. Someone was not bothering to move quietly.

"Let's go," Dino said. "Follow the noises."

They set off toward the sounds, away from the yacht club. The forest had been cleared of undergrowth here, and they could move quickly.

"If I hear weapons being cocked, I'm going to start shoot-ing," Dino said.

The noises stopped, and Dino held up a hand. There was a new sound. Someone panting. "I guess they were run-ning," he whispered.

"No lights yet," Stone whispered back. "I want to be able to see something before we pour more light on it."

"Okay. After you."

Stone crept forward. The brush was thickening. They must be on the property next door, he thought. "Stop," he whispered. He could hear the panting again, but he could see nothing. "The hell with it. Let's use the lights."

"You, first," Dino said.

"Thanks so much." Stone flicked on his light. Dino fol-lowed quickly. Something moved up ahead. "They're in black clothing," Stone said.

"Their weapons must be black, too," Dino replied. "Sweep right, slowly."

They panned their lights to their right. Nothing. "Back left," Stone said. They reached their first aiming point, then continued left.

"Oh, shit," Dino said. "Run for it!" He dashed past Stone toward the house, nearly knocking him down. "Cover me!"

Stone ran after him. "Yeah, sure."

They could hear their pursuers crashing through the wooded area behind them. Stone suddenly knew who was chasing them. He stopped and fired a single shot into the air, then pointed the flashlight into the woods. Someone was coming after them, moving quickly. Stone fired another shot upward. Dino stopped running.

"Bear!" Stone shouted.

Dino took off running again.

They made it to the porch and spun around.

"Where?" Dino said.

Then the back porch light came on, and they were blinded for a moment.

Dino adopted a combat stance, his weapon out in front of him.

"Don't shoot!" Stone yelled.

"Why the hell not?"

"First of all, you can't see the damned animal."

"How do you know it's a bear?"

"Panting, grunting, moving fast. And if you shoot it we'll have Fish and Wildlife down on us for a week, asking questions."

Dino backed up to the rear door. "I'm going to let you have the conversation with the bear," he said, ducking inside.

Stone backed up, too, but slowly. He didn't want to run for it then have the thing on his back. He stepped inside the house.

Primmy was standing there, her pistol in her hand. "Am I going to get another shot at them?"

"No, you're not. It's a black bear."

"Nonsense! There are no bears on this island."

"Once in a great while, one or two swim over from the mainland, sometimes in pursuit of a deer. I'll call Fish and Wildlife tomorrow morning, and they'll hunt it down, anesthetize it, cage it, and move it to a more suitable environment than my back porch."

"Good idea," she said, holstering her weapon.

Stone turned and looked at his guests: each was holding a handgun. "Well," he said, "this is the best-armed dinner party I've ever seen."

Then they were all looking out the window. The bear stepped into the circle of light from the porch fixture and walked around, sniffing things.

"He's got your scent, Dino," Stone said.

"Yours, too."

Then the bear turned and ambled off into the darkness. The phone rang, and Stone picked it up. "Hello?"

"It's Billy. We had a report of a bear near you."

"Too near. He just left my back porch."

"Did you shoot it? Someone heard gunfire."

"I fired a couple of rounds in the air to scare him off. It didn't work. He finally left of his own accord."

"How big?" Billy asked.

"I didn't get a chance to weigh him, but up on his hind legs, he looked about as tall as Dino."

"I'm taller," Dino said.

"I think a call to Fish and Wildlife in the morning would be a good idea, Billy. We don't want him eating any of the kids in the swimming class at the club. You might suggest they keep them indoors until they've caged him."

"I'll take care of it."

"How long since this happened?"

"Four, five years. Good night." Billy hung up.

Later, after the dinner party had dissolved, Stone and Primmy lay in bed, kissing and fondling.

"Which was scarier?" he asked her. "The bear or the twins?"

"The bear, when I thought it was the twins," she replied. "I thought they had come for revenge over the ear wound."

"I don't think they'll forget that," Stone said. "For the next few days, I don't want you to go anywhere alone."

"That's easy," she said. "I don't *want* to go anywhere alone. Maybe ever again."

"I understand your feeling."

"Wouldn't it be nice if there were a Fish and Wildlife for rogue people, in addition to bears? If we could just call them and they'd come, anesthetize them, put them in a cage, and take them away."

"Something like that exists," Stone said.

"Oh? What is it called?"

"It's called the criminal justice system. These two have already been there once, but I don't think we'll ever get them back there again."

"What's the alternative?" she asked.

Stone sighed. "That remains to be seen."

22

Early the following morning, Stone had an idea. He made love to Primmy (not a bad idea), they had breakfast, then they dressed and went downstairs. Dino and Viv were just finishing theirs.

"Dino," Stone said, "I've had an idea about how to go after the twins."

"Does it involve running around in the woods in the dark with flashlights chasing bears?"

"It does not. It involves police work, something you and I know a bit about."

"I thought you had forgotten," Dino said.

"Only when I can persuade you to do it for me."

"Is that what we're doing now?"

"No, we're going to call Sergeant Tom Young at the Maine State Police and persuade *him* to do it for us."

"I thought you'd already spoken to him, and he was unwilling to get involved."

"That's true, but you should always give a man a chance to change his mind."

"Okay, let's call him, and you do all the talking while I listen."

"That's what I had in mind." Stone led him to Dick Stone's little office, concealed behind a bookcase. "We'll use the landline and put it on speaker." They sat down, and Stone called the number.

"Sergeant Young."

"Tom, it's Stone Barrington and Dino Bacchetti."

"Uh-oh. You've hit a dead end on the Stone twins thing, and you're going to try to talk me into helping."

"We're not asking you to stick your neck out, Tom, just to review the unsolved rape/homicide files of the Islesboro cases, and those in Boston and New Haven."

"Hold it right there, pal," Young said. "I have already been over those cases with a giant magnifying glass, and there is nothing there that would help us make a case against the twins."

"Oh."

"Except, maybe, one thing."

"Ah. Which one?"

"Let's call it the Nantucket file, for want of a better name."

"What does Nantucket have to do with this?"

"It has to do with the twins' alibi for the last of the rape/homicides."

"What was their alibi?"

"They said they were on board a yacht that they had raced to Nantucket and were delivering to Boston."

"Did that check out?"

"At first. I had a local Nantucket cop, Lieutenant Jake Potter, run it down for me. He found the owner of the yacht, which is named *Hotshot*, on somebody else's yacht in the marina. When Jake spoke to him, he said that the twins had left Nantucket to deliver *Hotshot* to Boston, and the murder had occurred during the time when *Hotshot* would have been at sea. There would have been no way they could have gotten to Islesboro during that time, so their alibi was airtight."

"That's discouraging."

"That alibi was all that I knew at the time, but when I went through the files last week, there was an addendum to the file that I hadn't seen before."

"What did the addendum say?"

"It said that, after Jake had sent me the file, he had gotten a call from a kid he had wanted to interview but couldn't find. The kid delivered groceries to yachts in the marina. He had arrived aboard *Hotshot* as they were ready to cast off. He had handed the groceries aboard, got paid, and helped them stow everything below. It was a choppy day, and they didn't want loose cans of tomatoes flying around the cabin."

"So how does this relate to the twins' alibi?"

"According to this kid, there were four people aboard, and none of them were twins. He cast off their last line and watched them head out of the harbor."

"So they lied about their alibi?"

"Right, and the owner of *Hotshot* backed their lie, saying that the twins had sailed on her."

"Is that enough to charge them?"

"Wait, there's more."

"Tell me."

"Jake Potter checked the local airport to see if they could have left the island on a plane or chopper, and he learned that a small airplane left before *Hotshot* sailed."

"What kind of airplane?"

"A light, high-winged airplane. That's got to be a Cessna, but Cessna has several high-winged airplanes, and there are other manufacturers, too."

"Did Potter get a tail number?"

"No, they didn't buy fuel, so there was no record of a tail number."

"Anything else to add?"

"No, it's just clear evidence that they didn't sail aboard *Hotshot*, and that they could have left the island by airplane."

"That would be very nice if there were some physical evidence, like a murder weapon or DNA."

"But there wasn't. Oh, there's something else in the addendum that I didn't know before."

"What's that?"

"*Hotshot* is registered as having Boston as a home port, and the owner of the boat, who backed their alibi, is named Kip." He spelled it for Stone.

"Just 'Kip'?"

"He may have many other names, but that's the only one Potter got."

"Okay, Tom. Do you have any suggestion as to what we could do with this?"

"Not a one, except to stick the story up your ass if you tie me into this. And that means not tying in Jake Potter, either."

"So we're back to square one."

"Yeah, and the route from square one to an arrest is fogged in."

"Well put, Tom. Are you sure there's nothing else?"

"Not from me, there isn't. You're on your own. Bye." He hung up.

"Well," Dino said, "I'd call that convincing evidence."

"Yeah," Stone replied, "but the only ones convinced are you and I."

"I don't suppose anybody keeps a record of who lands at the airstrip on Islesboro."

"I hate saying these words, Dino, but you are absolutely right."

"So near, but yet so far."

23

Stone and Dino were crouched over the computer, trying to penetrate the website for yacht registrations, when Stone, after a half dozen attempts and without a password, had a better idea.

"I've got a better idea," he said.

"Yeah, sure. Remember what happened when you got your last idea, what, an hour ago?"

"We need the help of someone authorized, who can penetrate this website or, perhaps, do it the old-fashioned way and make a phone call. We need a tame cop."

"Yeah, but you only know one cop up here, and he's stopped helping."

"I was thinking of you."

"I'm not a Maine cop."

"The boat registration website is federal," Stone pointed out.

"I'm not federal," Dino pointed out.

"But you know lots of feds, don't you? All he has to do is call the number on the website and ask them to do a search for a yacht—that is, a sailboat named *Hotshot*, registered to an owner named Kip."

"Kip is not a name, it's a nickname. You think that the feds register yachts to nicknames?"

"Well, what name might be shortened to Kip?"

"Kissinger?"

"Nah."

"Kiplinger?"

"Nah."

There was a sharp rap on the door, and Stone opened it.

Primmy stood there. "You didn't tell me you two were hiding in the walls. Seth ratted you out."

"Come in," Stone said, pulling her inside and closing the door behind her.

"What are you doing?"

"We're looking for somebody who owns a yacht registered with Boston as a home port."

"Then you only have to search a couple of hundred thousand yachts. Do you have any filters?"

"What?"

"Filters. You look for a yacht. If you know its name, you enter that in the search thingie, and so on. It filters out everything that is not as you're describing it."

"Well, the name of the yacht is *Hotshot*, and we know the owner's nickname is Kip."

"Well, why didn't you just ask me?" Primmy said.

"You have the yacht registry tucked away in your brain somewhere?"

"No, but I know the yacht. And I know Kip."

"Yeah?" Dino asked. "What's Kip short for?"

"His name is K. P. Harwood. His friends just left out the *i*. He owns *Hotshot*, which is a custom-built Hinckley 54, probably paid for with his clients' money."

"And how do you know this?"

"Because Kip is my stockbroker, or was, until the feds got onto him for a few not-exactly-legal moves he was making. When I heard about that, I found a new stockbroker. Who needs her money tied up in a federal investigation for several years?"

Dino turned and looked at Stone. "Why doesn't she just conduct the investigation for us?"

"Well, she's doing better than the Maine State Police and the Nantucket Police Department and us, put together, isn't she?"

"Why don't you two just tell me what you want, and I'll see if I can help," Primmy said.

"Can you figure out where *Hotshot* is docked? We know it's in Boston."

"At the Fairwater Yacht Haven in Back Bay."

"She's like Siri," Dino said. "You just ask her, and the answer pops out. Where the hell is Back Bay?"

"Fairwater Yacht Haven is on the Charles River, down from Cambridge. You want directions? Nearby restaurants? Tattoo parlors? Cheap parking?"

"Wouldn't it just be easier to take her along?" Dino asked.

"I believe you may be right, Dino," Stone said.

"Second time today! Do you think a 1938 Ford woodie station wagon can get to Boston and back without putting us afoot on an interstate?"

"Seth keeps that car in perfect condition," Stone said.

"We should go now," Primmy said. "There's a race to Provincetown tomorrow, and everybody will be clearing the marina by eight AM."

"Do you think we'll find Kip there?"

"Kip never misses a race," she says. "When he's on the water, he's harder for the U.S. attorney to find."

"We'd better pack an overnight bag," Stone said. "Siri. Excuse me, Primmy, can you recommend a hotel?"

"Sure. What kind of hotel would you like?"

"One with thick walls," Dino said. "I don't want to spend the night listening to you two."

"I've got a better idea," Stone said.

"Now what?"

"Let's take my Cessna. We fly into Boston somewhere and rent a car."

"We'll still have to stay the night, in order to get to the marina before eight AM," Dino said.

"So what? We won't be on an interstate."

They landed at Hanscom Airport, west of Boston at mid-afternoon and drove into the city in a rental car. They checked into the small, but elegant, hotel that Primmy had booked.

"Here's a thought," Stone said.

"Uh-oh," Dino replied.

"I'll bet you Kip is sleeping aboard tonight, rather than getting up in the wee hours. Why don't we drop in to see him after dinner?"

They had dinner in the hotel restaurant, then drove to the marina.

"Where will we find the boat?" Dino asked.

Primmy went into a little shed, talked with a young man for ten seconds, then returned. "*Hotshot* is moored in berth G 12, right over there." She pointed.

"Lead the way," Stone said. Then he stopped them. "Primmy, we need some sort of wedge with Kip."

"'Wedge'?"

"Something we can tell him will happen to him if he lies to us, like going to jail."

"Tell him you'll haul his boat to investigate him, if he doesn't cooperate. He would miss the start of the race."

24

They trooped down the pontoons until they came to a handsome yacht where two couples were sitting in the cockpit, drinking beer.

"Hi, Kip!" Primmy said.

"Primmy! What brings you down to the sea? You coming back to me?"

"No, Kip. Let me introduce Mr. Stephen Barton," she said, slapping Stone on the back, "from the U.S. attorney's office. The other fellow is U.S. Marshal Dino."

"Aw, Primmy, not here! This is holy ground."

"This is salt water, or maybe brackish," she replied.

Stone spoke up, "Mr. Hapgood . . ."

"Harwood," Primmy said quickly.

"Mr. Hardwood, you see that crew over there by the travel trailer?" Stone nodded toward a half dozen workmen standing around, smoking cigarettes. "They're standing by to haul your boat—and a very pretty boat it is—"

"Yacht," Kip said.

"Yacht, sure, but it has the same destination, whatever you call it."

"What destination?"

"A yacht auction that starts at nine AM."

"*What?*"

"You heard him, pal," Dino said, flashing his badge too quickly for it to be read. "Speak up or cough up."

"What the fuck are you talking about?" Kip asked, feigning outrage.

Stone spotted fear under the outrage, and he knew he had his man. "We can do this the easy way or the hard way," Stone said. "The easy way, and you start your race tomorrow morning. The hard way, and you will be unavailable for sailing, since you will be in federal lockup. Your yacht will be sold at auction, with the proceeds going to the government. You still get to make the monthly payments, though."

Kip turned to his friends. "You mind going below for a few minutes so I can have a private conversation with this gentleman?"

His friends got up and shuffled below.

"Okay," Kip said, when they had gone. "What do you want?"

"We're checking on the veracity of some testimony you

have previously provided to a police officer—to wit, that, the day after finishing the Nantucket race, Eben and Enos Stone sailed aboard *Hotshot* for Boston and didn't arrive until that night."

"Yeah, what about it?"

"We now have two witnesses to contradict that testimony and say that you were lying. Answer this—and be careful to be truthful. There's a lot at risk here."

"Oh, all right."

"Did Enos and Eben Stone sail aboard that day or did they fly their airplane to Islesboro?"

Kip looked abashed.

"Tell me the truth, and we're outta here," Stone said. "Otherwise . . ."

"You want me to rat out two friends and clients, is that it?"

Stone cupped his hands and shouted toward the travel lift, "Okay, guys, crank her up. We'll motor over there!" He turned to Kip. "Let me have the ignition keys."

"Okay," Kip said. "I'll rat them out, but what do I get?"

"You get to keep your yacht and start the race tomorrow and not be charged as an accessory to rape and murder."

"They did *not* sail aboard this boat from Nantucket to Boston. They had their Cessna at the Nantucket airport, and I don't know where they went."

"Are you ready to testify to that in court?"

"Court?" Kip asked weakly.

"That's a good thing for you. They'll be in jail until the trial, not looking for you."

"I'll swear to it!" Kip said.

"Good. You are to keep this conversation entirely confidential. That means you tell *no one* about it, especially the Stone twins. Understood?"

"Understood," Kip said, nodding vigorously.

Stone yelled at the crew ashore again. "Never mind, guys!"

The men ashore shrugged and went back to smoking.

"Thanks for your time," Dino said. "We'll be in touch when we need you. Be sure to be available at all times, on a moment's notice."

The three walked back up the pontoon to their rental car. They waited until they were driving away before exploding in laughter.

"God," Primmy said. "I hope the U.S. attorney doesn't hear about this. You guys will be in terrible trouble!"

"Trouble? Us?" Stone said. "*You're* the one who said I was the U.S. attorney and that Dino was a federal marshal!"

Primmy looked stunned. "But . . ."

"No buts," Stone said, then he couldn't stand it anymore and started to laugh.

"I'm going to get you for that!" Primmy shouted. She held up her iPhone. "And you better be nice, if you want the recording of what Kip said."

"Peace!" Stone shouted. He got out his cell phone and called Sergeant Young.

"Tom Young."

"Tom, it's Stone Barrington."

"Not again," Young moaned. "What now?"

"I have a recording of an interview with Kip Harwood, admitting that the Stone twins did not, repeat did *not*, sail back to Boston on his yacht on the day of the last murder in Islesboro, and that they left Nantucket on their airplane!"

"No shit? And do you have testimony on where they landed and when, and when they took off again?"

"Not yet. I thought you might want the honor of wrapping it up."

"Yeah, sure, the honor! Nice try! Tell you what, you get me a written, sworn statement from Kip that puts them on Islesboro at the time of the murder, and I'll see what I can do."

"You're an unreasonable man, Tom. I'm giving you the cake. All you need to provide is the icing."

"You give me both, and I'll give you the knife to slice it with."

"I have to do everything around here," Stone muttered.

"Now you know how I feel!" He hung up.

"Well," Stone said, "it was worth a try."

25

Carly Riggs slid into her desk in class; Tim Scott was already in the next desk. "Are you ready?" she whispered.

"We're all set," he whispered back. "My car is on the right-hand side out of the front door, a tan station wagon. We'll leave separately and meet up there."

Somebody rapped sharply with a gavel, and the large room fell quiet.

An hour later, in the car, Tim turned down a dirt track and drove for half a mile. They emerged into a small clearing, hemmed in by trees on three sides and open to a beautiful view of the lake on the fourth.

They got out, and Tim retrieved a picnic basket and a

blanket from the rear of the wagon and spread the blanket on the thick grass. "Lonely enough for you?"

"Perfect," she said. They sat down on the blanket and kissed. "Don't you want lunch?" she asked.

"I want an appetizer first," Tim said, unzipping her jeans and pulling them off. The thong took only a second longer.

A few minutes later, they lay dozing, his head on her belly. They heard a car door close somewhere.

"What was that?" she asked.

"Don't worry about it."

"What if we're disturbed?"

"So what? They've probably seen a naked girl before."

"Ouch!" she said.

"What's the matter?" Then something stuck his back, and he didn't seem to care what it was anymore.

Carly woke first, just a little. She became aware that she was spread-eagle on a bed, her hands tied on each side and her legs apart, secured at the ankles.

"How was it?" a male voice asked.

"Sweet. It's a pity we can't save some for later."

"We need to get them out of here."

"I know. First, another shot."

Something stung her right buttock, then he moved away. "Him, too."

"Have you got the thing rigged?"

"It'll let in about a quart a minute. Nobody's out there at night."

Carly drifted off, before she could ask her question.

She woke up in cold water. Someone had her by the hair.

"Hang on," he said. "Can you help pull yourself up?"

She flailed with one arm and made contact with something wooden and slippery.

"Stay on your stomach," he said, "and hang on. We're about fifty yards from shore."

Carly held on for her life, while somebody rowed slowly. She faded again, and this time, she woke lying wrapped in a blanket. Someone brushed her hair out of her face.

"I've called for an ambulance," he said. "They should be here soon."

"Where's Tim?" she managed to ask.

"All I saw was you, just an arm draped over the gunwales of a sinking boat. I got hold of your wrist and held on. I'm sorry you were uncomfortable, but there's little room on a one-man racing shell. I like to come out here and row at night, when there's a moon. You don't have to deal with powerboats' wakes."

"You didn't see Tim?"

"I didn't see anything but your arm. Are you stoned?"

"Not in the way you mean. I was drugged, though." She felt herself drifting off again. "Tell them something for me."

"Tell who?"

"The ambulance people."

"What shall I tell them?"

"Tell them I want a rape kit."

"What?"

But she had already fallen asleep again.

This time it was daylight, and there was a whirring noise, as her bed sat up. Somebody put a glass straw in her mouth.

"Suck," a female voice said.

She sucked in water greedily. "I want a rape kit," she said, when she had slaked her thirst.

"Already accomplished," the woman said. "Your rescuer relayed your message."

"Where is he?"

"Around somewhere. He's only a teenager, but he got you aboard his shell and hauled you to shore."

"A friend was with me. Tim Scott."

"No word of him. Were you in a boat together?"

"I think so."

"You've been out for about nine hours. I've sent samples to the tox lab, and your rape kit is in the hands of the police."

"Thank you."

"Are you hungry? Would you like some soup?"

"Yes."

She pressed a button on the bed, and a nurse brought in a tray.

There were two cops; the woman did all the questioning. She had already asked for her name and address. "So you were in class. Tell me what happened after that."

"We had planned lunch together. Tim had a picnic basket in his car. He drove us out to the lake and to this little clearing. It was sheltered and had a nice view. We . . ."

"Did you make love?"

"Yes, sort of. He went down on me."

"Go on."

"I think we . . . me, anyway . . . I must have dozed off. Then I was stung by something, I thought a bee. Then he was, too."

"Was the sex voluntary?"

"Oh, yes."

"Then why did you request a rape kit?"

"It wasn't for him. I'm sore. I feel like I was penetrated."

"We'll know when your kit comes back. Do you think Tim did it?"

"No, I think Tim was out, like me. He was stung, too."

"Then you were taken. Both of you?"

"Yes, I think so."

"Do you remember what the man you saw looked like?"

"Two. There were two of them. They wore masks, like

surgical masks. They both had very blue eyes. I remember that. I heard them say a few words. I think Tim was raped, too. Is it possible he's still alive?"

"If he got out of the boat and made his way to shore. You were about fifty yards out."

"He wouldn't have left me. He's not like that. Where's the boat?"

"It went down. Tim probably went with it. They're out there, dragging the lake. Perhaps they'll find it."

"Are my clothes here?"

"No, you were nude when you were found."

"Let them know I had a handbag. I'd like that back, if possible."

"I will. I'll go make a call. You eat your soup."

Carly was torn between the soup and sleep. The soup won.

26

It was mid-morning a couple of days later. Everybody had finished breakfast, and most were reading the papers.

"Interesting piece in the *Times*," Lance said.

"I wouldn't be surprised," Stone replied.

"Is that your delicate manner of telling me I'm reading your newspaper?"

"I'm glad you thought it was delicate."

Lance folded the newspaper in such a way that the only thing Stone could see was the story and handed it to him.

"Thank you," Stone said, sipping a second cup of coffee.

"Aren't you going to read it?"

"Eventually. But, like a good host, I haven't prevented you from reading it, and you're going to tell me about it anyway."

"Oh, for Christ's sake," Lance said, "read the goddamned piece."

"Is it about the twins?"

"Possibly. You'll have to read it all to find out."

Stone unfolded the newspaper, to make a point, then began to read. He finished it, then looked at Lance, who was waiting for a reaction.

"It doesn't mention the twins," Stone said.

"Doesn't it? I thought they were all over it."

"You mean you think the twins kidnapped these two people, raped them . . ."

"Just the girl," Lance said. "There's no mention of rape with regard to the young man."

"I thought that was all over the piece," Stone said.

"You noticed that they were in a class before their little, ah, picnic?"

"Yes."

"You notice that the girl is a senior law student?"

"Yes."

"It would be interesting if someone rang them up and asked if they were in the twins' class on criminal appeals."

"I suppose they could have been," Stone admitted.

Dino, who had been reading his own copy of the *Times*, put it down and looked up. "I'm with Lance on this one," he said. "The story reeks of the twins."

"I suppose I caught a whiff of that," Stone said.

"You're just giving Lance a hard time. Stop it."

"Do you think Lance is contrite, for stealing my *Times*?"

"I am sorry," Lance said.

"But not contrite?"

"I refer you to the *Oxford English Dictionary*," Lance said. "I think you will find that the two words can properly be conflated."

"I'll take your word for it," Stone said.

"Does the story move you to action?"

"It's a moving story," Stone said. "What action do you suggest?"

"I think you and Dino should go to New Haven and interview the girl."

"We have no authority to do that," Stone said.

Lance checked his watch. "I believe you will have in a short while."

"How long?"

"How long does it take the FedEx truck to travel from the ferry to your house?"

"I suppose it depends on how many packages he has to deliver."

They heard a *beep-beep* from the front of the house, and Stone got up. He went outside and came back shortly. "It's for you, Lance," he said, tossing a book-size package to Lance from halfway across the room.

Lance caught it, took a small pocketknife from his

pocket, and opened it. Inside were two smaller packages. He tossed one to Stone, the other to Dino. "Congratulations," he said.

"For what?" Dino asked.

"A federal judge has appointed the two of you as United States Marshals."

Stone and Dino got their packages open. Inside each was a gold badge, a circle around a star.

"You will note that it does not say 'deputy marshal,'" Lance said. "It is the deputy marshals who do all the real work of the service, investigating, pursuing, arresting, and so forth. The marshals are people like you, honest but shiftless, who want to display some authority. You also have picture IDs."

Stone examined his ID. "This is my passport photo," he said. "I know, because I'm wearing a dinner jacket."

"Why did you wear a dinner jacket for a passport photo?" Dino asked.

"I was on my way to a dinner when I ran into a drugstore to have the picture taken."

"Now you have the authority to question victims of and witnesses to crimes."

"Murder is a state crime," Stone pointed out. "Why would U.S. Marshals have the authority to question a victim?"

"There were two victims," Lance said. "The young man was an FBI agent, finishing up a law degree at Yale. His last class was on criminal appeals. U.S. Marshals have the authority to question victims of and witnesses to federal crimes, and murdering an FBI agent is a federal crime."

"How do we know the guy was FBI? It's not mentioned in the story."

"I have other means of knowing it," Lance replied.

"I like it," Dino said. "Is there any way the use of this badge can come back to bite me on the ass?"

"Only if you commit a federal crime while wearing it," Lance said. "I suppose."

"Who was the federal judge who appointed us?" Stone asked.

"It's all in your commissioning document, in the envelope," Lance replied. "She's an old friend. Of the Agency."

Stone took this as a denial that Lance had had, sometime in the past, carnal knowledge of a woman who, later, became a federal judge.

"Well, now," Lance said, "I suppose there is nothing impeding your questioning the young lady in question. I've texted you her contact information, and I'll be dying to know what she has to tell you."

"I suppose," Stone said, "that being United States Marshals doesn't prevent us questioning her electronically, as on the telephone?"

"I suppose," Lance said. "That would obviate a trip to New Haven, wouldn't it?"

"It would," Stone agreed.

"If you would conduct this questioning by speakerphone, it would save you the necessity of relating to me what she said, or even of taking notes. Though a recording couldn't hurt."

"Let's make use of the cone of silence, shall we?" Stone said, leading the way to Dick Stone's little office. The three of them entered the office, followed by Lance, Primmy, and Viv, who arranged themselves while Stone dialed the number he had been given.

27

Stone called the number, and the phone was answered by a young woman.

"May I speak with Carly Riggs, please?"

"Who's calling?"

"This is United States Marshal Stone Barrington," he replied, "and my partner, Dino Bacchetti."

"You're from the press, aren't you?"

"I assure you, we are not. We are both duly appointed marshals."

"Do you think I'm stupid? I'm a law student, nearly a graduate, and every law student knows that Dino Bacchetti is the police commissioner of New York City."

"Would you like for Marshal Bacchetti to confirm his identity personally?"

"Yes."

Stone handed the phone to Dino.

"This is Dino Bacchetti. To whom am I speaking?"

"You're Dino Bacchetti, who I heard speak at Yale Law last semester, and you don't even know who you are calling?"

Stone handed Dino the paper with the woman's name.

"You are Carly Riggs?"

"I am. Why did it take you two guesses?"

"He's a little slow," Stone said.

"And you, you are supposed to be the buddy and former cop partner of Dino Bacchetti, the attorney?"

"That is correct. Also, a U.S. Marshal, duly appointed by a federal judge."

"And what is the name of the judge?"

Stone looked at Lance, eyebrows up.

"Elizabeth Prior," Lance said.

"And who was that speaking just now?"

"That was Lance Cabot," Stone said.

"Oh, the director of the Central Intelligence Agency? You must think I'm a complete fool."

"Your case has national security implications," Stone lied.

"Oh? How is that?"

"Are you aware that your missing companion, Tim Scott, is an FBI agent?"

"*What?*"

"He wasn't supposed to tell you that," Stone said.

"Now you expect me to believe that I could be in class

with the guy for a year, a guy I had been sleeping with, without finding that out?"

"As I said, he was not allowed to tell you."

"Why are we speaking of Tim in the past tense? Is he dead?"

"That is the assumption on which we are proceeding with this investigation."

"Do you have any evidence that he is dead?" she asked.

"Do you have any evidence that he is alive?" Stone asked quickly.

"Well . . ."

"We are proceeding on your testimony to a police officer that you were both kidnapped and were together in a sinking boat, from which his body has not yet been recovered. Though people are trying, as we speak."

"All right," she said. "Let's begin again, this time on the assumption that you three are who you say you are and not drunken practical jokers."

"I assure you that we are who we say we are, and that there are no drinking or practical jokes involved."

"All right, what do you want?"

"We believe that your case may be connected to other cases on which we are working, and we would like to hear your personal account of what happened to you from the time you left your class until you were pulled from the water."

"I would feel more comfortable if I could see your faces," she said.

"We are not in New Haven but in another state."

"We could accomplish that by using Zoom. That way, we will be able to see each other."

There ensued a quarter of an hour's discussion on how to use the app, followed by explicit instructions. Finally, everyone could see everyone.

"All right," Carly said. "I recognize Commissioner Bacchetti from his lecture and Mr. Cabot from newspaper photos, and you, Mr. Barrington, from a photo taken of you waltzing with the president of the United States. But who are the two women in the room?"

"One is Vivian Bacchetti, a retired police officer who is COO of a large security company. The other is a possible witness to a related crime. May we begin now?"

"All right," she said, then drew a deep breath. She launched into a detailed description of everything she could remember about her kidnapping and rape.

"So," Stone said, when she had finished, "there is nothing else you can tell us that would assist us in our investigation?"

"Well," she said, "how about the names of the two men who raped Tim and me?"

"You know them?" Stone asked, astonished.

"Let's say I recognized them," she replied.

"Please explain."

"The two men had the same startlingly blue eyes as each other, and the same eyes as the twins who conducted the criminal appeals class that I and Tim are taking. I believe they are Eben and Enos Stone."

"Let me understand you. Your identification of these two men is based entirely on the color of their eyes?"

"I suppose you might say that," she replied. "But they are uniquely vivid, identical, and exclusive to them."

"Did you tell this to the police?"

"No. When I talked to the police, I didn't yet remember where I'd seen them before."

"Ms. Riggs," Stone said. "You are a senior law student, by your own account. Can you imagine what a defense attorney for these twins would do to your testimony in cross-examination?"

"Well . . ."

"He would introduce expert witnesses who would testify that there are three zillion people with vivid blue eyes and that no one could identify a person on the basis of a few seconds' glimpse of his eyes."

"I suppose that's true."

"You say these men spoke to you when you were tied to a bed?"

"That is correct."

"Can you say, for certain, that their voices were identical to those of the twins who teach your class?"

"I suppose not. I hadn't made that comparison."

"Have you any other evidence to offer that would support your conclusion?"

"All right, I have not."

"Then I think we will not detain you further. We thank you for your time." Stone hung up. He was sweating a little.

"God help the courts when she starts practicing law," he said.

28

Carly Riggs put down the phone and wondered if she was having bizarre hallucinations associated with the drug she had been given. If so, that had been a very long and detailed hallucination.

There was a sharp rap at her apartment door. She walked rapidly toward it, then slowed and looked through the peephole, something she almost never bothered with. What she saw were the two detectives, a man and a woman, who had interviewed her after she was found in the lake.

She had forgotten their names. "Who is it?" she called out.

"Detectives Doris Spelling and Maury Miller. We spoke to you at the hospital."

Carly unlocked the door, let them in, and offered them seats in her small living room. The woman was carrying a shopping bag. "What can I do for you?" she asked.

"I'm afraid we've brought sad news," Spelling said.

"Is it Tim Scott?"

"Yes. We found the boat with Tim's body still in it. His parents have been notified and will be claiming the body."

"I'll write them a note," Carly said.

"That would be kind of you. Also," Detective Spelling said, holding out the shopping bag, "we found your clothes and handbag in a disused shed near the water. By the way, you were not in a lake but in the upper reaches of Quinnipiac River, where it is broad and may look like a lake. You were in East Rock Park."

"Thank you for clearing that up for me," Carly said, starting to go through the shopping bag.

"Are all your things there?" Spelling asked.

"Let's see: jeans, thong, shoes and socks, shirt, jacket. And my handbag." She looked inside. "They didn't take my money."

"Good," Spelling said.

"Tell me," Carly said, addressing Spelling's partner. "Why do you never say anything?"

"I'll answer that," Spelling said. "Because I tell him to shut up. He's new at this, and he'll learn more that way."

"You should ignore her and speak up anyway," Carly said to the man. "You won't learn much by not asking questions."

"Now," Spelling said. "Have you thought of anything else we should know since our first interview?"

"Yes, I've identified the kidnappers/rapists."

Spelling blinked. "How did you do that?"

"Wouldn't you like to know who they are first?"

"All right."

"Eben and Enos Stone, identical twins, who are teaching a class in criminal appeals that both Tim and I are taking." Carly told them about the eyes.

"Are you aware of the background of the twins?" Spelling asked.

"Yes, they were serving a life term for the murders of their parents, when they were pardoned by the new governor. In prison, they wrote a lot of successful appeals for prisoners, and since they had been Yale Law students, the college asked them to teach the course in summer school."

"Correct. Have you shared your views about the identities of your assailants with anyone else?"

"Yes, I had a phone call this morning from three men and two women . . ."

"Would these be Barrington and Bacchetti?"

"Plus, Mrs. Bacchetti and a woman they said was a possible witness in a related crime. And the director of Central Intelligence, Lance Cabot."

"We had a similar call from them," Spelling said.

"They said the twins were suspects in several rape/murders. Why weren't they doing time for those?"

"Because there was no conclusive evidence against them."

"Is what I've told you conclusive evidence of them raping Tim and me?"

"I think we might need more points of identification than just their eyes."

"Tell you what," Carly said. "If you'll stage a lineup of men with only their eyes visible, I'll bet I can pick the Stone twins out of it in short order."

"That's an interesting thought," Spelling said.

"You don't make it sound all *that* interesting."

"We have superiors who would need to be convinced of the usefulness of such a lineup. If you failed to pick them out, then it might damage our case at some point."

"I won't fail," Carly said. "Can you give me a phone number for Mr. Barrington?"

"Perhaps," Spelling said, flipping through her notebook. She read it out, and Carly memorized it. "Thank you," Carly said. "May I give you some advice?"

"That would be very interesting. Please do," Spelling said, as if to a child.

"If you will stop underestimating my intelligence and start using the help I've given you, you might wrap up this case a lot faster." She stood up. "Now, if you'll excuse me, I have a note to write to Tim's parents." She showed them out. Then she sat down and wrote a letter of condolence to Tim's parents; later she dialed Stone Barrington's number.

"Hello?"

"This is Carly Riggs," she said. "I'd like to come and see you. Where are you?"

"Why do you want to see me?"

"To help you solve this case. I'm sure you need the help."

"I'm on Islesboro," Stone said. "Do you want to fly to Islesboro? Do you want to come and see us?"

"Why not. How do I get there?"

"Drive to the New Haven airport, and look for a green and white Cessna 182. I'll be there in an hour. Bring a couple changes of clothing. I don't know when we'll get you back."

"Okay." Carly hung up, grabbed a duffel, and started filling it.

She parked and found a tall, good-looking man standing with another, shorter man next to a Cessna 182. Stone and Dino, she reckoned. They waved at her, then tossed her duffel and briefcase in the back and tried to put her in a rear seat.

"I want to sit up front," she said, "so I can see if you're flying it right."

Stone put her in the copilot's seat, Dino sat in the back, and shortly, they were airborne.

"Are you a pilot?" Stone asked.

"No, this is my first time in a small airplane," she said. "But I can tell you're doing it right."

29

S tone turned onto their final approach and set down the airplane. "Very good job," Carly said.

"I'm glad you approve," Stone said, taxiing to the ramp.

"I could have done that," she said.

"Actually, it takes a good deal of training to keep from killing yourself."

"I'm a quick learner," she said.

They got into the old Ford.

Dino spoke for the first time. "Anybody ever tell you you're a little on the pushy side?"

"No, but I've been told that I'm obnoxious."

"Let's not quibble over words," Dino said, getting a laugh from Stone.

They arrived at the house and found the ladies and Lance in the living room. Stone made introductions all around.

"I've already met you people on Zoom, remember?" Carly said. "Nice place," she said looking around the room.

"Thank you," Stone said. "Are you old enough to drink?"

"I'm twenty-four and a half, thank you. I'll have a bourbon on the rocks, please.

"Primmy," Carly said once they'd all been served and seated, "how do you fit into all this?"

"Primmy has had a personal encounter with the twins, resulting in her shooting one of them in the ear," Stone offered.

"The left ear," Carly said. It wasn't a question.

"Why do you think that?" Primmy asked.

"Because one of the rapists had a small bandage on his left ear. Here," she said, pointing at her own left ear.

"Why didn't you tell us that before?" Stone asked.

"It didn't occur to me. I just flashed on it when you said, 'ear.' Is that enough for a positive identification?"

"Probably not."

"I suggested to the two detectives from the New Haven police that they run a lineup with only the participants' eyes showing. I could make them that way."

"You sound very certain of yourself," Primmy said.

"I am nearly always certain. It's an annoying habit of mine."

"How did the detectives respond to your suggestion?" Stone asked.

"Oh, they brushed it off, said they'd talk to their boss about it."

"And they said it might harm their case, if you got it wrong."

"Right."

"The detectives were right, too."

"You used to be a cop, didn't you?"

"Right again."

"You don't look like a cop, but you sound like one."

"Okay, but Dino is better at sounding like a cop, because he still is one."

"You never get over being a cop," Dino said. "Stone still thinks like one."

"That explains it," she said.

"You seem awfully, well, together for a person who was drugged and raped about forty-eight hours ago," Primmy said.

"I was unconscious at the time, so I guess it didn't scar my psyche."

Primmy nodded.

"My guess is you and Stone are an item," Carly said.

"Good guess," Primmy replied.

"I knew I was right, or I would have already made a pass at him."

Stone choked on his bourbon. Everybody else laughed.

"Oh. Did you hear that they found Tim's body in the boat at the bottom of the river?"

"No," Stone said, "we hadn't heard that."

"The detectives told me. I've already written his mother a note."

"I'm sure she'll appreciate that," Stone said. "Does she know that you and Tim were, ah, an item?"

"Not unless he told her. We weren't exactly an item, though. More like friends with benefits."

"What's the difference?" Dino asked.

"An 'item' means it might get serious. Tim and I would never have been serious. I mean, he didn't even tell me he was an FBI agent."

"Maybe he was working on something you didn't know about," Stone said.

"Like what?"

"Maybe on the twins' case."

"He didn't mention it."

"If he was on a case, he wouldn't have."

"Well, at least he didn't lie to me," she said. "That would have been unlike him. Don't cops have to lie a lot?"

"We're allowed to lie to suspects," Dino said. "Sometimes it makes it easier to trip them up."

"I wonder if, when I get my degree, I should become a cop?"

"That could be useful, if you want to practice criminal law later in your career," Stone said. "It's what I did."

"When do you graduate?" Primmy asked.

"In a few weeks. I'm number one in my class."

"That's impressive," Dino said. He handed her a card. "When you get out, come see me in New York. I'll get someone to show you around the department."

"How long is the training?" Carly asked.

"The academy is six months, then you have field training, and you're on probation for twenty-four months, during which time you can get fired for any reason, so you have to watch your personal conduct."

"You want to see where the twins live?" Stone asked.

"Sure." She tossed back her bourbon and followed him to the MG.

"They're on the island," Carly said, getting into the little car.

"How can you tell?"

"I get feelings sometimes. They always turn out to be correct."

Stone gave her a tour of the island, and when they were driving out toward the point, she sat up straight.

"They live up here, on the right," she said.

He drove slowly past the twins' place, and Carly said, "This is it; they're watching from that window at the corner of the house."

"Can you feel that, too?"

"It's more than a feeling. I know it."

"Well, this time of day, the workmen are all gone. It could only be them there. I didn't see them, though."

"Neither did I—I just knew they were there."

"Spooky," Stone said.

"Yes, it is."

30

They were at dinner, and Stone and his friends couldn't get enough of Carly.

"Carly," Viv said gingerly, "are you on the spectrum?"

"Yeah, you noticed?"

"Well, there is the blunt speech."

"I have other quirks, too, like math."

"You're good at it?"

"I'm a prodigy," Carly replied. "Some of it in odd ways, like this afternoon at the twins' house."

"What was mathematical about that?" Primmy asked.

"The area. The square footage."

"That didn't come up," Stone said.

"It did with me. I could tell immediately that the house was 4,871 square feet in area."

"And how did you calculate that?" Stone asked.

"It wasn't a calculation," Carly replied. "It was just something I immediately knew at a glance."

"So, if we had the house plans and measured them, the area would be about that?"

"Not 'about that.' *That*," Carly said. "It's 4,871 square feet."

"How about this house?" Stone asked.

"It's 5,410 square feet," Carly said. "Not including the outbuildings. You've got another 2,200 square feet out there."

"To the best of my recollection," Stone said, "that is correct."

Primmy looked at her, askance. "You haven't been running around loose with a tape measure, have you?"

Carly laughed. "No, I haven't. I'm good at reciting peoples' heights and weights, too. I could make a fortune hustling at a carnival."

"Yet another career path open to you," Primmy muttered.

"Tell me, Carly," Stone said. "Why didn't you sense the presence of the twins when they came upon you and Tim by the lake?"

"Couple of things: I didn't have any interest in them beyond the class. And at that moment, Tim had been going down on me the previous twenty-nine minutes. I wouldn't have noticed a Mack truck approaching."

"What a good answer!" Primmy said. "Save that one for the courtroom!"

"Twenty-nine minutes?" Dino asked. "That's impressive."

"Tim was young and strong and incredibly fit," Carly replied, by way of explanation.

"I'll say," Viv commented.

"He had excellent stamina," Carly said. "But not much in the way of skills."

"Nobody's ever going to be able to say that of Dino," Viv said.

"Nor, I suspect, of Stone," Carly said with a giggle.

"In a minute, she's going to start divining dimensions of genitalia," Primmy said.

"I could," Carly replied, "and more."

"What an excellent time to change the subject!" Stone cried. "How was the game this afternoon?"

"There was no game this afternoon," Primmy said.

"Then what did you all do with yourselves?" Stone asked, growing desperate.

"It's all right, Stone," Carly said. "I won't embarrass you all. I know when to stop."

"I'll believe that when I see it," Primmy said.

Eventually, people began to stretch and yawn.

"Where would you like me to sleep?" Carly asked Stone.

"Well, the inside beds are filled. There are two guest-houses, with Lance in one. I don't think I'd feel good about you being alone in the other one."

"I'll be okay. Just loan me a shotgun."

"I think we'll just put you on the living room sofa," Stone said. He got a stack of linens and set them out for her. "There's a bath with a shower just off the garage. It's all yours, and there's a robe hanging on the back of the door. Would you like some very large pajamas?"

"If you'll loan me a Polo shirt, that will be a good length for me," she replied.

He went upstairs with Primmy, found a shirt and tossed it down the stairs to Carly, then he went into the bedroom and closed the door behind him.

"Maybe you'd better lock it," Primmy said.

"Stone?" The call came from downstairs.

"Yes, Carly?"

"Could I borrow that shotgun anyway?"

"I'll be right back," Stone said to Primmy. He went downstairs to Dick Stone's study, opened the weapons locker and loaded a riot gun for her, then took it into the living room.

"Do you know how to use a shotgun?" he asked.

"Not one like that."

He showed her how to load it, pump it, and the safety.

"If you hear a beeping noise in the night, it means someone is on the property. We heard that the other night. It turned out to be a bear. If you think it's a bear, don't go outside, call me. If it's a continuous noise, the intruder is in the house, or trying to get in."

"Got it." She yawned. "You'd better get upstairs," she said. "Primmy is waiting to show you that experience is better than youth."

Stone fled up the stairs. As it turned out, Carly was right.

31

Stone and Primmy came in a rush of yelling, laughing, and moaning. Stone rolled over on his back and took deep breaths. Primmy crept onto his shoulder and rested her head. "That was spectacular," she said.

"It was," Stone agreed. "It may have been even nearly fatal."

She listened to his chest. "Strong and steady. A good heart."

Then, from downstairs: "Stone! It's a bear!"

"I told her to call me if there's a bear," he said.

"I'm going to shoot her if there isn't a bear," Primmy said. "So go on downstairs."

Stone struggled out of bed and started for the door.

"Stone! Robe!" Primmy shouted. "Let's not confirm her estimates about you."

Stone got into a robe and slippers and started down the stairs. As he did, a shotgun went off—in the house. Stone resisted the urge to run down the stairs. "Carly?"

"Come on down, Stone," she said.

He walked on down and saw Carly standing, peering at the security system controls. "It didn't beep," she said.

Stone looked out the back picture window and saw it pockmarked in a tight circle by buckshot. He was impressed that the glass held.

"They were out there," Carly said.

"There were two bears?"

"Twins."

"Twin bears? That happens."

"The Stone twins! I took a shot at one of them, and they ran."

"You're sure it was the twins?"

"I felt them, then I saw them. They were dressed in black with masks, just as they were when Tim and I were kidnapped."

"Did the security system go off?"

"No, that's why I hesitated to fire."

"You didn't hesitate for long," Stone said. "I'll order a new window tomorrow."

"What's going on?" Dino asked from the stairs.

"We've had a visitation," Stone replied.

"Not a visitation, a visit!" Carly said. "There was nothing ghostly about it."

Dino walked over to the window and inspected it closely. "Looks like a couple of pellets got through. Did you fire more than once?"

"No."

"It's the ammo," Stone said. "It's a powerful load."

"Well, you might have put a couple of little holes in one of the boys," Dino said, admiringly. "Had you ever fired a shotgun before?"

"No. Stone showed me how."

"Well, you were right. You're a quick learner. I'm even more impressed with your intent than I am with your technique. Tell me, if you can remember, where he was standing. Where would you say the pellets struck him?"

Carly backed away from the window, examined it, and closed her eyes. "Upper chest, I'd say. Near the collarbone on his left."

Dino drew his weapon, switched on the porch light, let himself out the back door, and had a look around the porch. Then he came back inside, locking the door behind him. "No blood. I was hoping for a DNA match. That could have nailed them."

"Hey, you just reminded me," Carly said. "I asked the New Haven EMTs to do a rape kit on me."

"Did they?"

"Yes, but I don't know what became of it."

"I'll call over there in the morning and find out," Dino said.

"Everybody's heart rate back to normal?" Stone asked.

Everybody nodded. "Then let's get back to sleep. Nothing more we can do tonight."

"Tomorrow morning," Carly said, "I want to look at your system and find out why the warning didn't go off."

"Whatever you like," Stone said. Stone had, one way or another, used up all of the adrenaline in his body, and he climbed the stairs slowly.

Primmy was clurled up in a ball, sleeping soundly. That was okay with him. He shucked off the robe and got into bed as quietly as possible. In five minutes he was asleep.

The following morning Stone came down to breakfast to find Carly relating her story of the night before to Lance.

"Don't touch the electronics," he said to her. "I'll have my people do it from their end. They can run a diagnostic program."

"I can do that," Carly said.

"Not this program. It's proprietary."

"Oh."

Everybody sat down, and Carly gave them the short version of her story. After breakfast, Lance made a phone call. When he came back into the living room he said to everyone, "I want you to switch off all your electronic devices—phones, computers, vibrators—and I mean *off*, not just idling along. In fact, remove the batteries. My IT people are going to run some tests, and they don't want any interference."

Everyone complied. "Can we turn on the TV?" Dino asked.

"No, unplug it. The ones upstairs, too."

Soon they had achieved an electronics silence in the house.

"I didn't say you couldn't speak," Lance said. "So, unless you're electronically based, feel free."

The keypad for the security system began making a series of noises, once even playing a little tune.

"At least it isn't 'Daisy, Daisy,'" Dino said.

This continued off and on for the better part of an hour, then the computer played a farewell fanfare and was silent.

"All right," Lance said. "You may reassemble your devices." They did so. Dino plugged in the TV in time to get a news report that the missing FBI agent's body had been recovered from a sunken boat in the river.

As if on cue, there was a sharp knock at the door. Stone answered it, and two grim-looking men in suits stood there, holding up badges.

"FBI," one of them said. "Are you Stone Barrington?"

"Yes."

"Do you know the whereabouts of a Ms. Carly Riggs?"

"I believe I do," Stone said. "Please come in."

32

The two agents came into the living room. In their dark suits, button-down collars, and bland neckties, they looked like aliens from the spaceship *Federal*. They held up their badges.

"Good morning," the taller of them said. "I am Special Agent Neal Olshan, FBI, and this is my partner, Special Agent Robert Paul. Which of you is Carly Riggs?"

"I am," Carly said, giving them a little wave. "And no, you may not speak to me alone. I want witnesses."

Olshan looked a little worried. "I'm afraid we have to speak about some rather delicate, personal matters," he said. "Things they might not care to hear."

"They've heard it all before, with all the wrinkles and

crevices. And they've stood up to it very well. I hope you two can do the same. What do you want to know?"

"Let's start with your criminal appeals class," Olshan said.

"Would you like to sit down?" Stone asked, indicating two vacant chairs.

"Thank you, yes," the agent replied, then did so.

"All right," Carly said. She took them through her experience, step by step, omitting nothing and finished with her rescue from the river by the teenager. "There," she said finally, "anything else?"

"You have told others that you recognized your assailants."

"Rapists."

"If you prefer."

"Yes, I do. I didn't say I recognized them. I, rather, identified them from their eyes, which were uncommonly blue and identical, and from their manner of speaking."

"You recognized their voices?"

"No. I recognized their manner of speaking."

"And how would you describe their 'manner of speaking'?"

"Shorthand," she said. "They used very few words to communicate, and yet, both understood exactly what was said."

"I understand that you have said you could pick them out of a police lineup by their eyes."

"I did say that, and I'm waiting for somebody to take me up on it."

"We may well do that, if we can locate them."

"I believe you can locate them about a mile down the road, at their house," she said.

Olshan sat up even straighter. "They're on the island?"

"Are you sure?" asked Agent Paul.

"I believe I may have put a shotgun pellet or two into one of them last night, right over there on the back porch."

Both men got up, walked over to the window, and examined the marks left by the shotgun. "Is this armored glass?" Olshan asked.

"Ostensibly," Stone said. "You will note that only two pellets penetrated the glass. If the pane had not been armored, it's likely the better part of it would have shattered."

"Mr. Barrington, may I ask why you live in a house with armored glass?"

"It came that way," Stone replied. "I inherited it from a cousin who was a career CIA officer, and it is my understanding that it was built to the Agency's specifications."

"I can confirm that," Lance said.

"Mr. Cabot, is it?"

"It is."

"Do the specifications include a security system?"

"They do, but it did not operate as intended. Why, is being investigated as we speak."

"I see."

"What else do you see?" Carly asked. "I'd be grateful for your insight, if such exists."

"I believe you have drawn all the correct conclusions," Olshan said, "except for your untested theory about the police lineup."

"Then test it," she said. "I've told you where to find the twins."

"It's not the sort of thing that can be managed on the island. We would need the cooperation of the Connecticut and Maine State Police, and the use of one of their facilities. If we did it any other way, we would be liable for any failure of the test."

"Failure by me, you mean?"

"Well, yes, for want of a better word."

"'Me' is a perfectly good word, in the circumstances," she said.

"First, we'd have to arrest them, then . . ."

"I don't see why that's a problem."

"We must have a charge."

"How about the rape and murder of an FBI agent and the rape and attempted murder of his companion?"

"There are other considerations," Olshan said.

"Political ones?" Stone asked.

"Well, yes. The twins have already been pardoned by the governor for the murders of their parents. We understand that their father was a classmate and friend of the governor at Yale."

"Are you afraid that, if you arrest them, the governor will pardon them again?"

"There is that to consider," Olshan said. "My superiors are, ah, sensitive about such matters."

"Carly," Stone said, "I believe these gentlemen require a smoking gun."

"No gun was used."

"I speak metaphorically. They require better evidence than bright, blue eyes."

"Like DNA from a rape kit?"

Olshan looked really surprised this time. "A rape kit exists?"

"The examination was made," Carly said. "Last I heard, it was in the possession of the New Haven police."

"What lab was it sent to?"

"I have no knowledge of the lab preferences of the New Haven police."

"Then I think our next step is to run down that kit and its report."

"And would the rape kit constitute a smoking gun?" Carly asked.

"If it was properly conducted and the results properly examined, retained, and preserved under the proper circumstances."

"Tell me," Carly said, "do identical twins have identical DNA?"

Olshan looked at her blankly. "I have no idea," he said. "I'd have to research that."

Stone spoke up, "I'm told that the DNA of identical twins can have differences."

"What is the source of your information?"

"Impeccable," Stone replied, holding up his iPhone. "Siri."

33

The two FBI agents rose to leave. "Ms. Riggs . . ."

"Why don't you just call me Carly," she said. "Everybody else does."

"Carly, you mentioned that the twins are in residence at their home?"

"I did."

"Would you kindly show us where that is?"

Carly thought about it for a moment. "What kind of car are you driving?"

"A Chevrolet four-door sedan, a Malibu, I believe. A couple of years old."

"Does it have a government sticker on the door?"

"Um, I don't know," Olshan said.

"Does it have a government license plate?"

"We'll have to check," he said.

"I'll come with you."

They walked out to the car, which was as Olshan had described it.

"There," Carly said, pointing at a front door. "I believe that sticker identifies the car as government property." She walked around to the rear. "You gentlemen are not exactly undercover, are you?" she asked, pointing at the license plate, which read USGOVT, along with a number.

"Why should we mind if they know we're government?"

"Because you don't want them to know anything more about you than they already do."

Olshan looked around. "Where are we going to find other transportation on this island?"

"We'll borrow Stone's car," she said, and went inside for the keys.

"What's up?" Stone asked.

"These two doofuses want to tool around the island in a government vehicle with badges all over it."

He handed her a key. "Take the station wagon."

"Thank you." She went back outside. "Did you bring a change of clothes with you?" she asked Olshan.

"Well, yes. For downtime."

"Go into the garage and lose the suits, hats, ties, and white shirts, and put on the most casual clothing you have. Right now, you're the only people on the island dressed in suits and ties."

They got cases out of the trunk and went into the garage.

They came out wearing short-sleeved plaid shirts and khakis.

"Do you always wear wingtips with khakis?" Carly asked.

"Ah . . ."

"Do you have baseball caps?" Carly asked.

"Yes, but they have FBI on them."

"Let's pop into the village store and get you some better gear."

She drove them into the town and took them into the shop. "Hey, Billy," she said. "It's Carly, Stone's friend."

"Hey, Carly. Who are the two dweebs?"

"We need something that makes them look less dweeby."

Billy waved a hand. "Knock themselves out."

They left a few minutes later. Olshan wore a yellow V-neck sweater and a Sam Snead–style straw hat. Agent Paul wore a red windbreaker and a matching ball cap that simply read MAINE. And they both wore sneakers.

Carly stopped them on the way out and went over them for tags. "Now," she said, "you are presentable, which is to say, unnoticeable. Hop in, I'm driving."

Billy watched them from the front porch.

"Billy, you want to come along for camouflage?"

"What am I camouflaging?"

"Two obvious FBI agents."

She introduced them, and they all got into the car, Carly and Billy in the front seat.

"Are we supposed to be looking at real estate?" Billy asked. "Is that the idea?"

"Yep."

"Then why don't they have wives? No man looks at houses without his wife."

"They're gay," Carly said.

"Now wait a minute," Paul objected.

"For purposes of this excursion. You'll have plenty of time to deny it later."

Olshan burst out laughing.

"One of them laughs," Billy said, deadpan. "Here we go," Billy said as they approached the new property of the Stone twins. "Just pull into the driveway."

"We don't want to be obvious," Olshan said.

"Then act like a buyer."

Carly pulled into the drive and stopped short of the yard, where various pieces of equipment were moving around.

Billy got out of the car and stood in the group, pointing here and there. "Camden is up that way. Lincolnville, where you got the ferry, is down that way. And a couple of doors away lives a guy named Ed Rawls, who's ex-CIA, with his girlfriend. If you approach his property in an untoward way, he'll shoot you where you stand. Remember that."

Billy turned back and pointed at the house. "They've

skinned it back to the bones and are starting over. The electrical and plumbing work is nearly finished, and the plastering is underway. The twins live in a big room on that corner of the house. They brought in enough furniture to make themselves comfortable. Any questions?"

"Can we take photographs?" Agent Paul asked.

"Sure, as long as your gear isn't professional-looking."

"How about with an iPhone?"

"Fire away."

Paul took a dozen photos, and they got back into the car.

"All right," Billy said. "Now we get a tour of the island."

"I'm not sure if we have time before the ferry," Olshan said.

"Unless you want your cover blown, act like a normal person," Billy said, pointing at an upcoming house. "Primmy Primrose lives right there."

"We met her at the Barrington house," Olshan said.

"Yeah, she's afraid to stay at home with the twins hovering."

"Everyone is being very respectful of the twins," Olshan remarked.

"Shit-scared would be a better description," Billy said. "Those boys were pulling the heads off small, furry creatures when they were six. Everybody has been scared of them ever since. I've never seen the island relax the way it did the day they started their prison term. Now, they're all tense again."

"I'm negatively impressed," Paul said.

"Me, too," Olshan commented. "Make a note, Bob, we go armed at all times while we're here."

"Don't think you're safe off the island," Billy said, "if they take an interest in you."

"Let's see that they don't," Olshan said.

"Too late," Carly replied. "All you can do now is just try to look harmless."

34

They drove past Primmy's house, then on past the Jacksons' place.

"Hang on," Billy said. "Pull over here."

Carly did so. "Something wrong?"

"I just want to take a look at something." He walked back down the road a few paces and peered over the hedge at the Jacksons' house, then he went back to the car and got in.

"Anything wrong?" Carly asked.

"Yes." Billy got out his phone and called Stone.

"Hello?"

"It's Billy. I'm out with Carly and the two FBI geeks, and we just passed the Jacksons' place. Their car is sitting out front, and the driver's door is open. Has been for two days, now."

"Wait for me. I'll be there as soon as I can."

"What does the car door being open mean?" Olshan asked Billy.

"It means they haven't closed it. Do you leave your car outside with the door open?"

"No, now that you mention it."

"We'll wait for Stone and Dino before we go in."

"Do they have some expertise that we don't?"

"Probably. They were both homicide detectives with the NYPD. Dino is the police commissioner down there."

"I should have recognized the name," Olshan said.

Stone's MG appeared in Carly's rearview mirror. Both cars pulled into the Jacksons' driveway. Everybody, including Lance Cabot in the back seat, got out and followed them.

"Pretty place," Olshan said.

"It used to belong to the Stone family. The twins murdered their parents here," Billy said.

"Spooky vibes," Carly said. "You guys go first."

Stone found the front door ajar, and he pushed it open. "Henry Lee? Grace?"

"You won't get an answer," Carly said.

The group walked into the living room and found Henry Lee and Grace Jackson, posed in chairs at either end of the sofa, each with a pistol in hand and a neat hole in their foreheads.

"Jesus God," Lance said. "How could this happen to these people?"

"Who are they?" Olshan asked.

"They're both CIA officers," Stone said. "They work for Lance, and they're here to help us with the Stone twins case."

"Did the twins have something against them?"

"They bought the Stone family house before the twins could bid," Billy said. "I knew the boys were pissed, but I never expected anything like this."

"All right," Stone said, getting out his phone. "Everybody back out of here, just the way you came in, and wait on the front porch."

"You need some help working the scene?" Olshan said.

"We're not going to work the scene," Stone said. "We'll leave that to the Maine State Police. Maybe it will get them interested in the twins again." He made the call to Sergeant Tom Young. "Tom? Stone Barrington. We've got a double homicide for you, staged to look like a murder-suicide or a mutual suicide. At the Stone family house. Dino and I and two FBI agents will wait for you on the front porch. Take the helicopter and bring everybody." He hung up.

To Stone's surprise, Lance took a silver flask from inside his jacket and took a swig from it. "Sorry," he said. "I'm used to reading about my people dying, but I've never witnessed the aftermath." He looked shaken.

It took just under an hour before Tom's crime scene team arrived on the front lawn; they didn't bother with the airfield. As the chopper wound down, the doors opened and people carrying equipment and cases spilled out and followed Sergeant Young into the house. Stone and his party stayed on the porch, leaving the others to it.

"Shouldn't you FBI types be taking an interest in this?" Carly asked Olshan. "After all, CIA officers are federal employees."

"There are enough people in the house," Olshan said. "We'll leave them to make their conclusion, then we'll get copies of their reports. It will go faster that way."

Eventually, Tom Young came out of the house and collapsed into a porch chair. "Well," he said, "I don't buy either of the suicide stories. As far as we're concerned, it's a straight-up double homicide."

"I concur," Dino said, and everybody else nodded. "And your suspects are right across the road."

"No, they're not," Billy said. "The twins left on a morning ferry. I don't know where they went."

Stone checked his watch. "And by this time, all the workmen have left the site. You won't have anybody to interview until tomorrow, Tom."

"A day late, and a dollar short," Tom muttered.

"Not your fault," Stone replied. "We came upon them by accident. Billy noticed an open car door."

"It's the little things that matter," Tom said.

"You'd better check your people into the inn," Stone said. "Billy, have they got rooms?"

"They've got four," Billy replied. "Two are booked through the weekend. Shall I book you in?"

"They'll give you dinner there, too," Stone said.

Tom nodded. "Thanks."

"Do you need us for anything else?" Stone asked.

"We'll get your statements tomorrow," Tom replied.

"Well, let's get home, then." Stone got up and led his party to the station wagon and the MG.

Back home, Stone said, "I'll bet that somebody besides Lance could use a drink."

"Hell, yes," Dino said, and everybody else nodded. He explained to Viv and Primmy what had happened.

"Stone," Primmy said, "you're stuck with me until those boys are dead."

"I'd better leave in a day or two," Carly said. "I've got graduation ahead of me. So I've got to pack and ship my things somewhere and get Tim's car back to his parents."

"Do you have a car?" Stone asked.

"With my first paycheck on my new job," she said, "wherever that may be."

"Do you still want to practice law, or do you want to be a cop now?"

"I worked hard for that degree. I'll stick with the law."

"I understand that you interviewed with my firm, Woodman & Weld, a few weeks ago."

"Yes, I guess I interviewed with at least a dozen."

"Had any offers?"

"Two or three. None that I particularly wanted."

"Woodman & Weld were impressed," he said. Stone wrote a name on his business card and handed it to Carly. "Call Herb Fisher tomorrow. You'll be starting a week from Monday as an associate. You'll spend your first couple of weeks in bar exam class with the other new associates, and you can bunk at my house until you've had a chance to look for your own place."

"You can just snap your fingers and do that?"

"Well, no. You started the process with the firm when the recruiters visited Yale. And you and I have had a pretty extensive series of conversations. I've talked it over with Herb and our managing partner, Bill Eggers. Everybody's enthusiastic."

"Wow," she said. "It seems you've taken the trouble to solve all my problems at once."

"You'll be starting a new life. You'll have plenty of problems to solve on your own."

The following morning, the Maine State Police homicide detectives came to Stone's house and took statements from everybody. Lance made arrangements for the Jacksons' remains to be shipped home to Georgia.

Stone called on Ed Rawls for a conversation he had known was coming.

35

Stone went through the two security gates, one of them a heavy log. He found Ed Rawls seated on his front porch with Sally, his British girlfriend. Sally was shelling peas into a bowl on her lap, while Rawls guarded her with a scoped long gun across his. Sally finished her peas, brought them coffee, and went back inside.

"She doesn't want to hear conversations like this one," Rawls said.

"How does she know what they're about?"

"She's known since the beginning that this was going to happen, but she's been waiting for it to become inevitable."

"Do you think it's inevitable, Ed?"

"I wouldn't be wasting a nice evening on you, if I thought

it wasn't. Way I see it is, you've tried everything you could honorably do to resolve this situation, and now you're left with the dishonorable alternative."

"You think it's dishonorable?"

"On paper, yes, but not really. They've backed us into a corner, so there's nothing else left for it. Also, I think they're coming for me next."

"Why you?"

"Apparently, they don't like having neighbors. They went after Primmy and failed. Now with the Jacksons, to my surprise, they succeeded. I knew the Jacksons well back when, and in those days this could never have happened."

"I guess you can sneak up on anybody," Stone said.

Ed looked straight at him. "We're about to prove or disprove that theory," he said.

"What are our chances?"

"Not good," Rawls replied. "They've got that house wired up backward and forward. I've counted eighteen security cameras, and I probably missed a few."

"They went ashore yesterday. I guess they'll have to come back," Stone said.

"They came back last night on the late ferry," Rawls said. "Now they're hunkered down in there, waiting to see what's going to happen."

"You think they want us to make the first move?"

"Not necessarily. I think they enjoy the prospect of what's

coming, and they don't need a first move from us to make them happy about taking us out."

"Can they see us now?"

"Not unless they're out on the water," Rawls said. "From my present position I can't see a security camera, so they can't see me, but they could just be sitting out there on the bay, waiting for us to twitch wrong. I'm happy to have Sally in the house, safe and sound."

"How good are your defenses?" Stone asked.

"As good as one skilled man—me—can make them, but maybe not good enough."

"Are you going to give them the first shot?"

"Sometimes, if you want somebody bad enough, it's the only way. At least, I can control the circumstances, to some extent."

"I think you ought to pull inside and wait for dark," Stone said. "Loan me a weapon, and I'll wait with you."

"That's not a bad thought," Rawls said. "I think I'd prefer having you here than someplace else."

"We've got Dino and Lance, if we need them."

"Four is too many," Ed said. "Just you and me are about the right number. Come on." He led the way inside, where they found Sally shucking corn, while keeping an eye on the monitors connected to a dozen high-definition cameras, covering the house, the road, and the dock. "What's your pleasure?" Ed asked, waving an arm at a weapons rack.

"Something with a silencer, but long enough to take them at a distance. I don't relish close combat."

"Not when the opposition is that young, that big, and that strong—and there's two of them." He handed Stone a rifle with a silencer and a banana magazine. "That holds thirty rounds," Rawls said, "and you can set it for single fire, double, triple, or auto."

"I think I'd like double," Stone said, twisting the knob.

Rawls handed him an ammunition crate filled with loaded banana magazines. "If you run out of that, you're a bad shot," he said.

"Where do you want me?"

"There's a firing slot cut into that wall behind you," he said. "It will give you a wide field of fire that will overlap with mine."

Stone found it and set up a chair, then put his rifle across it.

"Supper will be ready pretty soon," Ed said. "I think we can rely on my security alarms until then to tell us they're coming."

"They managed to disarm my alarms through the computer system, to Lance's chagrin. He thought the Agency's system couldn't be penetrated, but they managed it."

"I'm sorry to hear that," Ed said. "I don't think my system is any better than Lance's."

"He's got his people working on a way to get into their system," Stone said. "Maybe that will be of some help to us."

———

A few minutes later, Sally called them to supper. It was fried chicken, peas, sweet corn, and biscuits.

"Sally's been working on cooking Southern," Ed said. "She's getting good at it."

"I like it myself," Sally said.

There was a tiny noise from somewhere. Ed stopped eating and listened for a moment. "Just the house settling a little," he said.

"It does that sometimes," Sally agreed.

"Ed, did you restock those rocket-launched grenades?" Stone asked. "I think we used them up the last time we were in a situation like this."

"I've got three," Ed replied. "That sort of materiel is hard to come by up here. I have to wait for out-of-town visitors."

"Would one of those burn them out?"

"It would knock a corner off their house, but I don't think an RPG would torch it, unless, of course, there was a propane tank involved."

"Where is their propane tank?"

"Buried on the other side of the house."

"Oh."

"Yeah."

36

Viv, Carly, Primmy, Dino, and Lance sat in Stone's living room, having an after-dinner cognac. Lance's phone purred.

"Yes?" He listened for a moment. "Are we going to have this problem again? Is that the best answer you can give me? It better be." He hung up. "Our security system has been reprogrammed, rebooted, and is now operational."

"For how long?" Primmy asked.

"Don't be a cynic, Primmy."

"Your questions sounded pretty cynical to me," she said.

"I have to sound that way for effect sometimes." He thought about that. "Sometimes I think that half of what I say is for effect."

"What is Stone doing right now?" Carly asked.

"Probably what we're doing," Dino said. "They'll be fully battened down, though."

"I think I've just fully realized that Tim is dead, and I'm not," Carly said.

"Would you have it any other way?" Dino asked.

"I'd rather have both of us alive."

Dino shrugged. "You have to take things as they come. Change them, if you can, but that can take a while."

"Oh, Dino," Viv said. "You always sound so wise on your second brandy."

"Cognac releases my wisdom," Dino replied.

"Sometimes," Viv said.

Stone, Sally, and Ed had finished dinner, and Ed was checking a gunport. "Uh-oh," he said.

Stone grabbed his rifle and went to his own port and peered out. "What's that?" he asked.

"Flashing lights," Ed said. "Like on a police car."

"The only police cars on the island arrived after Tom Young came in on the chopper."

"Well, they're up and running," Ed replied. "Here they come, and they're cuffed."

Stone looked out the port and thought he saw the twins being bundled into a car. "What will they do with them? The ferry's down for the night."

"I expect they've got other transportation," Ed said. "A boat, or better still, their chopper." As if responding, rotors could be heard turning. "They're choppering them to their office. Let's go." He got up and opened the door.

"Go where?" Stone asked.

"I'm tired of staring at the outside of that house," Ed said. "I want to see the inside."

They got into Ed's car and drove up to the house, which was brightly lit from indoors and out.

"You don't suppose they have help in there, do you?" Stone asked.

"Who'd help the sons of bitches?" Rawls said. "Anyway, they've always done everything alone together." He parked the car, and they got out. Ed walked up the front stairs.

"What about their security system?" Stone asked.

"I doubt if Tom gave them time to set it. Anyway, who'd hear it if it went off?"

"We would," Stone said, covering his ears while Ed fiddled with the front door. It came open. "Not locked," Ed said, then walked inside.

"Right behind you," Stone said, following. They were first in a short hallway, then in what would, no doubt, be the living room. The smell of drying plaster was thick.

"Let's take the ten-cent tour," Rawls said. They went into the kitchen, the dining room, and into what would be a library or study, all with drying plaster. The library had rows of bookcases lined up and ready to be installed.

There was a broad central staircase, and Rawls led the way upstairs. "Hello? Anybody home?"

"I won't fire until you do," Stone said.

Rawls turned a corner and went through an open door. "And we're in the master suite," he said. It was only partly furnished, but neat.

"Interesting that there's only one bed," Stone said.

"Two," Ed replied, "twins pushed together, inside a king bedstead. And electric beds, like at a hospital."

French doors led out to a long, narrow porch on the side facing the road, wrapping around to the front of the house, then again, to the library.

"Pretty good field of fire from up here," Rawls said, noting the relative positions of his house, porches, and dock.

They went back inside, and Ed opened a glass-fronted cabinet. Inside was a row of assault weapons and racks for handguns, plus shelves for ammunition, of which there was plenty.

"They're prepared for a siege," Stone said.

"More likely a slaughter," Ed said.

They walked around the house once more, just to imprint the floor plan in their minds.

"How long you figure before they're completely moved in?" Rawls asked.

"Well, let's see," Stone said. "The HVAC systems are

working, the kitchen cabinets and appliances have been installed, and the plastering is complete, if not yet dry. The study cabinetwork has yet to be installed, and there will be at least a week of painting. I'd say two to three weeks, if they're hurrying."

"That's about what I figure," Rawls said.

"Why do you ask?"

"I'm opportunity oriented," Ed said. "I look around me now, and what I see is opportunity, gradually vanishing as each job gets done."

"Maybe the Maine cops have got something on them in the Jackson murders," Stone said. "Something we missed when we walked around the crime scene."

"I hope so," Ed said. "That would sure make life easier for all of us."

"I can't hang around the whole summer waiting for a chance to exercise my right to self-defense," Stone said.

"I'm less pressured and more patient than you," Ed said back.

"I can't argue with that. Do you have a plan?"

"Several. Outlines, of course; not fleshed in. Ways of approaching the job."

"What do you think is the better plan?"

"I think we have to kill them before the house is finished," Rawls said. "Can you stick around that long?"

"Probably not," Stone said. "But I'll do the best I can."

"That's good enough for me."

37

Stone slept in Primmy's arms, and they amused each other both at bedtime and on rising. They joined the others for breakfast, where Stone told them all of the previous evening's events and their tour of the Stone twins' house.

"Is it nice?" Primmy asked.

"It's going to be, when they're done."

"Maybe I'll buy it when they're dead," Primmy said.

"I think that's a better plan than making an offer now. That way, you don't have to deal with the twins, just Billy Hotchkiss."

"Billy's a piece of cake," Primmy said. "Especially if his client is dead, like the twins are going to be."

"Primmy," Stone said, "do you know something I don't know about the twins?"

"Perhaps."

"Would you share it, please?"

"In due course," she said. "I've already shared it with Carly."

Stone looked across the table at Carly. She was looking smug, he thought.

"Don't worry," Carly said, "it's a good thing."

"As long as it isn't detrimental to the health of the rest of us," Stone said.

"Shouldn't be," Primmy said.

Stone's phone rang. "Yes?"

"It's Ed. The twins are still not back; you want to do a little nautical reconnaissance with me this morning?"

"Sure."

"Come on over here as soon as you like."

"Can I bring the others?"

"As many as you like."

"See you in half an hour." Stone hung up. "How many of you want to take a ride on Ed Rawls's boat this morning?"

Primmy's and Carly's hands shot up. The Bacchettis exchanged a meaningful glance, which Stone knew meant sex. They wanted the place to themselves.

"I'll come along," Lance said.

"Fifteen minutes, in the station wagon."

Thirty minutes later they were clambering aboard Ed's motorboat as the morning sun warmed them. Stone took a seat next to Ed, who was at the helm.

Ed accelerated and turned north toward open water. When he had gone a couple of hundred yards, he spun the boat around and cut the throttles to idle, taking her out of gear.

"There," Rawls said. "Nice view of my house, huh?"

"Very nice," Stone said. "What are we doing here?"

"Assume we're in the house, and the twins are out here: How could they best kill us?"

Stone peered at the house, then picked up some binoculars. "Day or night?"

"Make it easy on yourself."

"Okay, if it's night, I can probably see us sitting at the table or up and walking around."

"In daylight?"

"I'd need us to come outside. Easy shot, if we're outside in daylight."

"I can't argue with that. You see the porch table?"

"Sure."

"That's three-inch thickness of Maine heart pine, well-seasoned. You tip that on its side, and you've got a good barrier between us and a shooter out here."

"Granted."

"Let's remember that the next time we're on the porch. We can just leave it tipped on its side. Saves time, when you're ducking bullets."

"I hear you."

"Now, let's take a look at their place," Ed said, putting

the engines in gear and pushing the throttles forward. Soon they were off the twins' dock. "You can see why they chose that room facing the road as the master bedroom."

"No shot from here at someone in the room," Stone said. "A whole other thing, if you're on the road. Or you could set up on the Jacksons' upstairs porch, facing the road."

"You could make life very hot in the twins' master from that vantage point," Rawls said.

"I like it better than shooting from the seaward side," Stone said. "I'd feel a whole lot more comfortable on the Jacksons' porch."

"So would I," Ed said. "What's in that room off the porch?"

"Guest room, I think. Twin beds."

"Right. If we're going to set up a shooting gallery, I reckon that's our spot."

Lance came and sat next to them. "I have the distinct feeling," he said, "that you two are up to no good."

"You want some of this, Lance? There's room on the Jacksons' upstairs porch for another man with a long gun."

"It's been a long time since I shot someone in the head from a distance," Lance said. "And, as I recall, there were no policemen within a hundred miles."

"Fond memories," Rawls said.

"And anyway, my chopper is coming for me at three this afternoon."

"Do you think you could drop Carly off at the New Haven airport?" Stone asked. "She has a car there."

"Of course. Anything for a citizen, especially one as pretty as Carly." Lance smiled. "And my blessings upon your little shooting party."

They were back at Ed's house for lunch, where Sally had prepared a huge steak and kidney pie. They fell on it.

Carly came and sat down by Stone. "Are you trying to get rid of me? Lance says he's giving me a lift."

"I'm happy to have you here as long as you like," Stone said. "I can fly you over to New Haven in the Cessna, whenever you like."

"If you don't mind, I'll stick around for a bit."

"What are you and Primmy cooking up?"

"Let's just say we can't pull it off in New Haven."

"You aren't going to get yourselves killed, are you?"

"That is not part of our plan," Carly said.

"The two of you are driving me nuts."

"I know," she said.

38

Shortly before dinner, Stone had a call from Sergeant Tom Young. "Yes, Tom?"

"Sorry to call with bad news, Stone," he said.

"Let's have it."

"I had hoped to keep the twins on ice with a high bail, but they saw a judge this afternoon, and he released them on their own recognizance."

"Shit," Stone muttered.

"I hear that the judge had a call from the governor before the bail hearing," Tom said.

"Where are they now?"

"On their way home. They'll make the last ferry."

"Thank you, Tom. Good night." Stone hung up and called Ed Rawls.

"Speak to me."

Stone broke the news.

"Well, shit!"

"Same here. Tom Young says they'll make the last ferry tonight."

"That's good information," Ed said.

"Does that give you an idea?"

"You don't want to know. See ya." Ed hung up.

Dino was looking questioningly at him from across the table.

"Why are you looking at me questioningly?" Stone asked.

"Lance has left us. Somebody had to."

"I know nothing. Ed wanted it that way."

"Hearing that is almost as good as knowing something."

"If you say so."

Ed checked his watch. It was nine-thirty. The last ferry arrived at eleven. Plenty of time to arrange something. He went into the living room, where Sally was knitting something unidentifiable, opened a panel in the wall, unlocked a cupboard door, and looked inside at the array of ammunition and explosives. He chose a block of C-4 plastic explosive, about four ounces, he reckoned, some radio-initiated detonators, and a small radio. That should do it, he thought. He strapped on a pistol, retrieved a light machine gun and four magazines, and dropped the lot into a canvas carryall.

"Traveling someplace?" Sally asked.

"Only a short distance. I'll be back in less than half an hour."

She nodded. "Go safely."

Ed thought about taking the boat, but since nobody was at home at the twins', there was no need for stealth, so he'd hoof it. He walked outside, looked around, and listened. Gorgeous, starry night; a loon nearby calling to its mate; cool, dry air: Maine at its glorious best. Given their latitude, some daylight lingered in the western sky, so he didn't need his flashlight. He walked to his fence and let himself through a gap that no one else would have seen. He found himself waist-deep in blueberry bushes, and walking was slow going.

He reached the border of the twins' property and walked across a graveled area. Paving stones were stacked on pallets in large numbers; there would be a cobblestone parking area and driveway in a few days. He looked toward the twins' dock and saw where the teak boardwalk began. There was a large, square floating dock that would take three or four small boats, then a further boardwalk to a final floating dock that would accept a fifty-footer. The depth out there would be six feet or more at low-water spring tide.

Ed walked up the front steps. There were still lights on inside; nothing had changed since his and Stone's earlier visit. He stopped and listened intently. Nothing, except the distant sound of rotors from a helicopter far out on the bay. He walked on upstairs and into the master bedroom.

He set the carryall on the nearest bed and used its remote control to raise the head to its steepest angle, which gave him a view of the mechanics and electrical connections of the electric bed. He took the chunk of plastique, ripped off a foot-long piece of duct tape from its roll, and taped the explosive to the rod that moved the bed. He selected a detonator from his bag and pressed it into the explosive, which had the consistency of modeling clay. Finally, he returned the bed to its fully down position and set the remote control back where he'd found it. Then he heard the helicopter rotor again, this time from much closer. It occurred to him that the twins might not have bothered with the ferry; they could have flown directly from the Augusta airport to the island. If that were so, he knew where it would land.

Ed grabbed his carryall, quickly let himself outside onto the surrounding porch, ran to the corner of the house, and peeked around it. A small helicopter was setting down on the square floating dock. Two figures alit from the copter and began walking up the floating boardwalk toward the house.

A quick look around ascertained for him that he could not leave the house anywhere except on the side facing the road. He was looking for a place to jump where a landing might not break a leg, when he heard heavy footsteps on the front stairway and the sound of the front door opening.

Ed considered just flinging himself off the elevated porch into the darkness and hoping for the best, but he reconsidered. They were coming up the stairs to the second floor now. Ed crept around the corner and began moving around the house toward the corner of the porch facing the sea. He had to go slowly for fear of making a noise.

He caught a glimpse of the twins' backs as they turned toward their bedroom, then he continued, now walking faster.

Then he heard a voice. "Is that your duct tape on the floor by the bed?"

"No," came the reply.

Ed reached the end of the porch and saw a drainpipe coming down from the roof. He swung a leg over the railing, dropped his carryall, grasped the drainpipe, and slid down it like a fireman answering an alarm, making some noise in the process.

He knew he couldn't run through the blueberry patch, so he ran for the floating boardwalk, dashed down it to the pontoon, and launched into a dive. A split second before hitting the water he heard a shout from the house, but he couldn't tell what was said. He dove into the black water and swam for the bottom, which happened at about four feet. He swam along it, waiting for the gunshots to find him, but nothing happened. He swam past the outer floating dock, bobbed up long enough to grab a breath, then went down deeper. He reckoned he had eight feet now, but he couldn't hold his breath much longer, what with the exertion.

Then, above his head, the water began to explode.

39

Ed swam, his lungs bursting, until he bumped his head hard on the hull of his boat. Breathing hard, he pulled himself along the deck to the stern, where there was a boarding ladder. Arriving there, he realized that he had left the dock lights on and one of them hung directly over the boat, illuminating every square foot of it.

Ed breathed hard for another half a minute, to get enough air into his lungs to shout, then he hollered,

"Sally!" No response. Once more. "Sally!"

She opened the door wide and stood there, sheltered from the view from the house next door. "Ed?"

"Turn off the dock lights, then the inside lights, and stay low and well away from the windows."

"Done!" she shouted back and closed the door. A moment later the dock lights went off, then the interior lights. Ed, who was freezing now, pulled out the boarding ladder built into the stern, climbed up and over, and lay in the darkened cockpit, heaving in air and trying to gain strength. Finally, he was able to crawl forward through the saloon and down the companionway ladder to the head below, where he showered off the salt water and rubbed himself down with a thick, dry towel. Then he shucked off his wet clothes and wrapped the towel around himself, waiting for what remained of his body heat to warm him.

That done, he found a change of clothes and got into some khakis and a polo shirt, dry underwear and socks, and a spare pair of Top-Siders. He found a bucket and stuffed his wet clothes into it, and tossed it into the cockpit. He crawled back up the stairs and into the saloon, where he found a bottle of whiskey, poured himself one, and sat on the floor, drinking it and pondering his circumstances. He had one more lap to run in this race: from the boat, up the boardwalk, across the front porch, and into the house, where the thought of a warm woman waiting helped him recover his strength.

He transferred his pocket things from wet to dry pockets, then he realized that somewhere, on the run or the swim over, he had lost his 9mm auto from its holster. He made his way back below, and using his flashlight, lifted the mattress on the double bunk, tapped in the combination of the safe there, and retrieved a .380 pistol and another belt and holster. He strapped it on, secured the safe, and crawled back above.

He resisted the temptation of another drink, since he had to be able to run another twenty yards pretty quickly. Finally, he peeped over the instrument panel and at the twins' house. Nobody on the wraparound porch, nobody visible inside.

"What the hell," he said aloud to himself. He stood up, grabbed the bucket and carryall, then placed his other hand on the gunwale and vaulted onto the dock. He ran and simultaneously yanked the small pistol from its holster. He made the porch and stood with his back flat against the front door, panting. The door was locked. He knocked sharply on it. "Sally? Open up!"

He heard the latch work, then the door opened, and she yanked him inside by his belt. They wrapped around each other. "Don't ever scare me like that again," she said.

"I'll work on that," he replied.

"You need a drink."

"You're right."

Still keeping low, they both had a drink.

"The lights are off over there," Sally said, getting to her knees and looking toward the twins' house. "I expect they've gone to bed."

Ed got up, closed the blinds, and turned on one small

lamp. Then it came to him: the twins' bed. He emptied his carryall, fished around, and came up with the little radio controller for the detonators. He took a breath and pushed the button. Nothing. The little red light had not illuminated. Well, the thing had just taken a swim in salt water, hadn't it?

He found some batteries, tossed the old ones, then went into the bathroom and rinsed the radio thoroughly, then pointed the hair dryer at the radio until it was dry and warm to the touch, then he inserted the fresh batteries. Waited a minute. He wanted to see this happen. He went back into the living room, switched off the lamp, then pulled back the curtains. "Watch this," he said to Sally. "I hope they're in bed." He pressed the button on the radio. The red light came on and stayed on. Nothing else happened. "Shit!" he screamed.

"What's wrong?" Sally asked.

"The house was supposed to explode."

"Well, that was uncooperative of it, then."

"The duct tape," he said.

"What duct tape?"

"I dropped it in the hurry to get out. They found it and figured out what it was for."

"What was it for?"

"To hold a block of plastique in place under their bed." The phone rang and Ed grabbed it, half expecting it to be the twins. "Yeah?"

"It's Stone. Is something supposed to happen?"

"Yeah," Ed replied, "only I fucked up, and in a big way."

"Explain, please."

Ed explained.

"I thought the pros knew to clean up after themselves when they've left a bomb under somebody's bed."

"I believe they covered that in explosives class, but in my haste not to get shot, I neglected to check off that box."

"I take it you didn't get shot?"

"No, but I had to slide down a drainpipe, run thirty yards, dive into sixty-degree water, then swim in the dark over to my dock, none of which I'm in shape for. I'll spare you the rest of the details."

"Did your controller get wet?"

"Yes, but I dried it."

"Well, at least you're okay."

"Sure, but now the twins have four ounces of C-4 in their possession, and I have a feeling they're going to figure out how to use it."

"Well, they're not going to figure out how to use it to-night, so you might as well get some well-earned rest. That's what I'm going to do."

"What a good idea," Ed said, then hung up.

"I suppose that was Stone," Sally said.

"Yes, and he didn't berate me."

"You took care of that yourself."

"Do you think you could get my clothes off and get

me into bed?" Ed asked. "Because I think I'm going to col-
lapse."

"One of my favorite things to do," she said, and began to
work at it.

Three minutes later Ed was snoring.

40

The following day, Stone flew Carly and Primmy to New Haven for Carly's Yale Law commencement. Once on the ground, Stone put them into a cab. "I have a stop to make," Stone said. "I'll catch up with you."

Stone took another cab to a location where he had earlier made a purchase over the phone. His package was ready, and he headed for Yale.

The graduates were lined up in their black gowns with blue sleeves and filing into the building. He found Primmy and they managed to get seats.

"We thought you were going to miss the ceremony," she said. "Carly was nearly distraught." Primmy pointed. "There she is!" Waves were exchanged.

Stone had not been to a graduation since his own from NYU, and he had forgotten how exciting they were for the graduates. They listened to speeches, including Carly's valedictory address. Then the thing broke up, and Stone took them out to the parking lot. He handed Carly a key. "You drive."

"Drive what?"

"Right there." He pointed to a metallic blue BMW convertible with the top down. "Happy graduation!"

Carly nearly killed them twice on the drive to the airport. Stone arranged to leave the car in a hangar until she came back for it, then they boarded the Cessna and flew back to Islesboro.

"Let's take a look at the island," Stone said, dropping to about two hundred feet. He made some gentle turns, and one took them past the Rawls place and the twins' house, just down the road. The driveway was being paved with cobblestones, and two painters' trucks were parked out back. "Looks like finishing touches," Stone said.

"Let's get away from here," Primmy said. "I have the feeling they can see who we are."

Stone turned for the airfield and set down.

Back at the house there was a bottle of champagne and a good lunch waiting for them.

"I'm a lawyer now," Carly said.

"Well," Stone said, "there is a little thing left called the bar exam. Pass that, and you'll get your license."

"I didn't tell you, but I took the Connecticut exam last month and finished in the top one percent, so I'm already licensed in Connecticut."

At lunch, Primmy leaned over and whispered to Stone. "Did you see the Stone twins at the commencement ceremony?"

"They were there?"

"Yes, sitting in a section reserved for faculty."

"I'm glad I didn't see them. Did Carly?"

"I don't see how she could have missed them."

"Well, it doesn't seem to have lessened her elation."

"Were you elated when you graduated, Stone?"

"Was I! I felt free for the first time in my life. Then I went and joined the police force."

After lunch, the phone rang, and Stone answered. "Yes?"

"It's Rawls. I thought you'd like to know the twins, who I thought left this morning, are back."

"They were at the Yale Law commencement," Stone said, "but their airplane wasn't at the airfield when we landed. We circled their place and didn't see them, but it looks like the work is getting closer to being done."

"Then they'll be here all the time," Ed said. "I don't think Sally can take that. I'm going to have to move her, at least for the summer."

"You've still got your place in Virginia, haven't you?"

"Yes. They won't know about that."

"I guess we'll go back to New York this week," Stone said. "Carly is starting at Woodman & Weld next Monday, prepping for the bar exam. By the way, she and Primmy have cooked up something to do with the twins, but they won't tell me what."

"I don't know what to say to that," Ed said.

"Neither do I, but I expect we'll find out this week."

"I don't think Sally knows, or I would. She can't keep a secret."

"Primmy and Carly are all too good at it. When I ask about it, all I get is blank stares."

"Well, good luck to you. I'll let you know if anything breaks over here." Ed hung up.

"Listen, you two," he said to Carly and Primmy. "I need to know what you're up to."

"No, you don't," Primmy said. "I'll give you a hint, though, if you promise not to ask any further questions."

"Oh, all right, I promise."

"When we do it, it has to be done naked."

Carly burst out laughing. "The perfect clue!" she said.

"By the way," Primmy said, "are we going to see Ed Rawls anytime soon?"

"We can," Stone said, holding up the car keys. "You can take the MG, but you have to call Ed and tell him you're coming and be told how to get in."

Primmy snatched up the keys. "Done. What's his number?" She went into the next room and made the call, then returned. "Come on, Carly. We have to go see Ed."

The two drove away in the MG.

Primmy and Carly sat down with Rawls on the front porch and told him what they had in mind.

"That's very interesting," Rawls said. "I think I can work with that, if I know when this is to take place."

"Is half an hour's notice enough?"

"I suppose so. I'm concerned about your safety, though."

"We'll be just fine," Carly said. "We'll be armed, if it comes to that."

"My guess is you haven't told Stone."

"Good guess. Why make him nervous?"

"You mean, make *me* nervous, instead."

"Nah, you don't get nervous, Ed. You're the coolest guy we know."

"I'll keep telling myself that," Ed said. "Have you given any thought to the aftermath of your plan?"

"Yes," Primmy said. "We thought we'd let you take care of that part. After all, what more can we give?"

"That's one way of looking at it," Ed replied.

41

Billy Hotchkiss sat at his desk with the newspapers stacked up beside him and read his way through the day. Billy was the captain of his ship, as well as of his soul, and he was highly experienced at manipulating the controls from his desk. He only had to rise rarely. Today was one of those occasions.

Just before lunch he watched as the Stone twins, Eben and Enos, entered his shop and, with a nod of greeting to him, began to browse. Billy knew the twins enjoyed being thieves, so he always kept a careful eye on them and, as soon as they left, added whatever they had taken to their account. This time, to his surprise, they spoke to him.

"Good morning, Billy," one of them said, he wasn't sure which.

"Good morning," he replied, giving them his full attention.

"We need something in the way of electronics," the other twin said. "But we're not sure what it's called."

"Well," Billy said, "I've got cell phones and game boxes and like that. What do you want it to do?"

"We want it to transmit a signal to a receiver," the other said.

"You mean, like a two-way radio?"

"Yes, like that, except we don't need to speak, just transmit."

"Transmit what?" Billy asked, intrigued now.

"A signal."

"Yeah, sure, but what signal? You'd need a frequency."

"Right, exactly."

"What frequency do you want to transmit on?"

"We're not sure, so we'd like to transmit on a range of frequencies."

"Well, a marine VHF radio transmits on twelve or thirteen frequencies. Would one of those do?"

"It might. We've got one on our boat we could experiment with, I guess."

"Take a look at your receiver," Billy suggested. "It should have a frequency stamped on it."

"Not this one, I'm afraid."

"Okay, here's what you do. You get online and look at what's available in two-way radios. An aviation VHS would have a lot more frequencies on it than a marine radio. If you can't find exactly what you want, look for a customer service phone number, call them and ask for advice."

"That's a good suggestion, Billy," they said, simultaneously.

"Also," one of them said, "we need a box—make it two boxes—of Snickers bars. You're almost out."

"Let me check the storeroom." He did so and returned with two boxes of the candy bars. "Charge them to your account?" he asked.

"Yes, please."

He handed them the candy in a shopping bag, they left. Billy marked down both the Snickers and the alkaline batteries they had stolen. Then he called Stone Barrington.

"Yes?"

"Stone, it's Billy. Got a minute?"

"Sure, Billy."

"I just had the Stone twins in here, and they had an odd request." He related the substance of their conversation and the advice he had given them. "That make any sense to you?"

"Billy, let me make a call, and I'll get back to you."

"Oh, one other thing: they bought two boxes of Snickers candy bars."

That stopped Stone in his tracks. "That's ominous," he said.

"I remember when their daddy bought them by the box."

"So do I," Stone said. "Do you know if anybody on the island is missing? Women, I mean."

"No."

They both hung up.

Stone called Ed Rawls.

"I had your two girlfriends down here," Rawls said. "They're hilarious."

"What did they want?"

"They told me if you asked me that to tell you to go fuck yourself."

"I'll consider myself told," Stone said. "Now, here's a problem for you." He told Ed about his conversation with Billy. "Any idea what they're up to?"

"Yeah, I do," Rawls said. "They're trying to get ahold of a radio that will communicate with the detonator on the bomb I left at their house, and I hope to God they don't find one. Or, if they do, that they try it out while holding the explosives to their ear."

Stone laughed. "What are their chances of coming up with the right frequency?"

"Poor or none. I built that radio, and I didn't use a frequency that comes on a commercial radio. I hope they keep experimenting with it, though."

"Me, too."

"Their best bet would be to get on the Internet and find a unit that will broadcast on a broadband of frequencies, one at a time. It would be like trying to break into a safe with an electronic lock by firing hundreds of frequencies at it, until one works."

"Gotcha. Why don't you just build another one and explode it for them?"

"Because I can't remember the frequency," Rawls admitted. "Call it an extended senior moment."

"Work on it," Stone said.

"By the way, I like the plan your girls came up with. I'm happy to participate."

"Participate in what?"

"Nice try, pal, but you ain't getting nothing out of me."

"Just tell me this: Are the girls going to get themselves killed while carrying out their plan?"

"Not if I have anything to say about it," Ed said.

"Are you going to have something to say about it?"

"You bet your sweet ass, I am," Ed said, then hung up. Stone called him back.

"Now, what?"

"I didn't tell you about the Snickers bars."

"You're right. Why would you?"

"The twins bought two boxes of Snickers from Billy a few minutes ago."

"I'm sorry, I'm drawing a blank on this one," Ed said. "Why should anybody care if they've got a sweet tooth?"

"Remember when a certain lady of our acquaintance was kidnapped and held by their father?"

"Yes, I do."

"All she was fed while he had her was Snickers bars."

"Jesus Christ, is anybody missing?"

"Billy says no, and he usually knows what he's talking about."

"I don't know what to say," Ed said.

"I'll keep you posted."

They both hung up.

42

S tone stared at the phone, and his mind reeled. "Dino!" he shouted.

Dino came downstairs. "Yeah?"

"Where are Primmy and Carly?"

"They went out more than an hour ago in the MG. Don't you remember?"

"Yes, and they're not back?"

"Let's have a look around," Dino said, and they began searching the house and the property.

"Where's Viv?" Stone asked, when they came back in after a fruitless search.

"In the bathtub."

"For how long?"

"One never knows with Viv and the tub. Hours, sometimes."

"Bring her ashore and get some clothes on her. We're going to have to search the island, and I don't want to leave her here alone."

Stone pulled out of the driveway and drove through the village looking for the MG and the women. Nothing. He turned down the road toward Ed Rawls's house, then called Ed's cell.

"You again?"

"Primmy and Carly are missing."

Ed digested that for a moment. "Where are you?"

"In the station wagon, pointed your way."

"We'll follow you as you pass. First stop has to be the twins' house."

Stone slowed down, and as they passed Ed's front gate, the log rolled back, and Ed's Range Rover fell in behind the wagon. Stone's cell phone rang. "Yes?"

"Are you armed?" Ed asked.

"Handguns only."

"Stop."

Stone pulled over. Rawls got out of his car and walked to the station wagon, carrying two rifles and some magazines in a canvas bag. "Here," he said, thrusting them through the Ford's window. "I want them back when they're dead." He turned and walked back to his car.

Stone handed the weapons to Dino and Viv. "Load these," he said, tossing the bag into the rear seat. They were coming up on the twins' place now.

Ed flashed his lights, and Stone stopped and watched in the mirror as Rawls walked past his car, shoving a magazine into his rifle and working the action.

"Stay in the car," Rawls said as he walked past, "but cover me."

It seemed to be lunch hour for the workmen; all was quiet. Stone and Dino got out of the wagon with rifles and stood behind the car, looking toward Ed's figure.

"I'm going in!" Rawls shouted back at them.

"Bad idea!" Stone called back, but he and Dino took up positions.

Rawls never slowed down. He marched up the front steps and stood in the open doorway. "Stone twins!" he shouted. "Show yourselves!"

"Don't go in there," Dino muttered to himself. "They'll have an excuse to shoot you."

Rawls disappeared into the house, and they stood waiting for something to happen. Rawls appeared on the second-floor balcony and walked its length, looking into rooms, then he disappeared back inside. He was gone for two or three minutes before he emerged on the front porch again, shaking his head. He walked over to where they stood. "Nobody home," he said.

"Is there a basement?"

"Yeah, and I checked it. Empty, except for mechanicals. I think our next stop is the Jacksons' place."

They got back into their respective vehicles and turned down the Jacksons' driveway. The front door was ajar.

"Where's their car?" Dino asked.

"Billy put it in the barn," Stone said.

They all left their cars and walked into the Jackson house. They searched room by room, upstairs and down but found nothing. The barn contained the Jacksons' station wagon, but little else.

"The boathouse," Rawls said.

"That's where they kept her," Stone replied.

The path had been cleared and the walkway repaired. As they approached, the boathouse looked inviting, with its fresh coat of paint.

"Second floor," Stone said, and they went upstairs gingerly. The rooms were unfurnished, but clean. There were new kitchen appliances. "Not here," Stone said.

"Let's check around the dock," Ed suggested, and they went back downstairs. Still nothing.

They went back to the house, and as they entered Stone saw, down the center hallway, a flash of green drove past on the road.

"Who was that?" he asked.

"Could have been the MG, but I couldn't see the occupants," Dino replied. "It was too fast."

"Come on!" They got back into their vehicles, got turned around, and headed down the road to the village. They were past the store when Stone saw the MG turn into his driveway. He skidded through the turn and followed it.

When they arrived at the house, Primmy and Carly were climbing out of the MG, cheerfully waving at them.

"Where the hell have you two been?" Stone asked, exasperated.

"Wherever the hell we wanted to go," Primmy replied in the same tone.

"Everybody calm down!" Viv said. "We've been searching for you, Primmy, and we were scared."

"We went down to see Ed for a while," Primmy said. "Then we drove down to the point and took a walk. It's nice down there."

Stone took a deep breath. "Primmy," he said, "new rules."

"What are they?"

"No one leaves the house without either Dino or me," he said. "And we all go armed. Come inside. We have some things to tell you."

They marched into the living room, where Mary was setting the table for lunch.

"First, the Snickers bars," he said.

"Snickers bars? You've gone absolutely bonkers," Primmy replied.

43

Everybody was quiet at lunch, until Primmy spoke up, interrupting everybody's half-nap. "Why are Ed and Sally not joining us?" she asked.

"In the circumstances," Stone replied, "he wants to stick close to home."

"Why is he safer there than here?" she asked.

"There, he knows that when he walks through the front door, there won't be two guys with shotguns waiting for him."

"I see. What's Ed's story? I heard you or somebody say 'ex-CIA,' but that's all."

"That's correct. Ed had thirty years or so, as an operative and station head. One of the best, by all accounts. Then he made a mistake."

"I'll bet 'mistake' is spelled 'w-o-m-a-n.'"

"You'd win money on that bet."

"Details, please. And dirt, too."

"Okay, after a long and extraordinary career, Ed was serving his out-the-door-and-into-his-pension posting as station chief in Stockholm."

"Uh-oh, Swedish woman."

"That would have been too smart," Stone replied. "Ed took up with a senior Russian diplomat's wife, true love and all that."

"Oops."

"You betcha, oops. They were caught in flagrante delicto in a hotel suite that had thoughtfully been equipped by the KGB with high-definition video and audio equipment. Although I'm told the footage was highly complimentary of Ed's skills, the Russians were more interested in what he knew while operating vertically, and they pressed him hard for that. Ed was too smart to give them anything but what a secretarial intern might have, but the Agency turned one of the KGB boys in Stockholm and he brought along Ed's home movies as a bargaining chip, as well as for the entertainment value. The Justice Department was inclined to go easy on Ed. But he, inevitably, had made a few enemies at the Agency on his way up the ladder, and they wanted him to take a hard fall, rather than have a soft landing."

"Poor Ed."

"Indeed. He got twenty years. Fast-forward a few, and he performed—from prison, mind you—services of considerable value to the country. Plus, when the Soviet Union collapsed, the Moscow station got a look at what the KGB had got from Ed, and it was laughable, almost a service to the country. There was a move afoot for a new trial, but that would have taken a long time, so the president gave him a full pardon. His time-in-service was restored, as was his pension. And though he still had enemies at Langley, he made a new life for himself. His marriage was gone, of course, but he managed very well. The Agency sometimes still employs him for special-mission stuff."

"Is that what he's doing now?" Carly asked.

"Let's just say that my cousin Dick Stone was a highly valued intelligence operative and executive who was about to move into the deputy director for operations job, the second highest in the Agency, and they did not take the murder of their fairest-haired boy lightly. They do harbor a vengeful streak that, at times, rears its head."

"Did the twins murder Dick Stone?" Carly asked.

"Without conclusive evidence to back me, I take the view that they did. Nothing I learned at the time or since has made me doubt my conclusion for a moment."

"That's good enough for me," Primmy said. "I'm aboard. Do with me as you will."

"Same here," Carly said.

"I understand that you two and Ed Rawls have already made a plan."

"We have nothing to say about that," Carly replied.

"Well, before you two go charging off into the Valley of Death, I'd like to know if you are fully aware of the dangers attendant to so doing. I mean, it's not called the Valley of Death for nothing."

"We are fully aware," Primmy said, "and we are confident of walking away from this with our heads firmly attached to our shoulders."

"Cannon to the left, cannon to the right," Stone said.

"Nevertheless, neither snow nor rain nor sleet nor gloom of night will stay us from the swift conclusion of our appointed duties."

"That is a misquotation and a horribly chosen metaphor," Stone said. "But I'll take your word, such as it is, and trust Ed Rawls to keep you alive."

44

As bedtime was approaching, there was a ring of the front doorbell. Stone checked the peephole. Ed Rawls stood there, a rifle slung over his shoulder and Sally at his side. Stone let them in.

"Sorry to drop by so late," Ed said. "But something's afoot with the twins."

Stone hustled them into the house and gave them each a drink. "What's up?"

"The twins. We drove into the village to get some ice cream, and when we left, their boat was tied up at their dock."

"Is that somehow sinister?" Stone asked. "Am I missing something?"

"What we're missing is the twins. When we got back to

our place I saw their boat headed out and turning south toward the point."

"What's to the south that should make us wary here?"

"Well, if they go around the point, then head north, what's in their path is the cove right out there—and more to the point, your boat and your house."

"I'm sorry, Ed, I was a little slow on the uptake."

"That's all right. It occurred to me that, if they're headed here, we might have an opportunity to catch them trespassing. And if we do, we've got a legal right to take a shot or two at them. I brought my nightscope," he said, patting the rifle.

Dino stepped up. "I'd like some of that," he said.

Stone got the men rifles from Dick Stone's weapons trove and they pocketed loaded magazines. "Why don't we wait for them on my boat," Stone said.

"Will it stop a bullet?"

"Hinckley says their hulls are bulletproof. There's Kevlar in them."

"Their boat's a Hinckley, too," Ed said. "The new one with three outboards. I expect their hull is made of the same materials."

"Are we living in a Hinckley commercial?" Dino asked. "Or can we go shoot at these people? Just for the fun of it, of course. No harm intended."

"Save it for the state police, Dino," Ed said. They moved down to Stone's dock.

"How do you want to do this, Ed?"

"Well, if I had my druthers, I'd set up a cross fire, but only one position is available to us: your boat."

"We should have surprise on our side," Stone said.

"Always a good idea," Ed replied.

They climbed aboard and made preparations.

"I'd like them to take the first shot," Stone said. "I prefer provocation to straight-up assassination."

"Tell you what," Ed said. "When they get close, you stand up, wave your arms, and call them dirty names."

"That's provocation," Dino said.

"Not if you're not shooting at them, it ain't. Listen, I got no problem at all taking the first shot, and if I do I'm planning to hit something, like somebody's head."

"Ed," Stone said, "I think we've got to get a positive ID on them before we start shooting people in the head. I'd hate to find out later that we murdered a couple of fishermen, returning home late."

"Picky, picky, picky," Rawls said. "All right, both of you know these boys on sight, do you not?"

"We do," Stone said.

"Then I'm going to rely on you to identify them. I won't fire until the two of you agree it's the Stone twins. Will that do it for you?"

"I think I can defend that position in court," Stone said.

"What court?" Ed asked. "Nobody's going to be alive to testify against us."

"We've still got to convince Sergeant Tom Young that we were in the right."

"All right," Ed said. "What's our story? It's better we're agreed on that instead of making it up later, in separate rooms with separate cops."

"You came over to the house and reported the twins leaving their dock and turning south. We speculated on their destination, and all three of us voted for right here. Okay so far?"

"That works for me," Dino said.

"We thought they might be coming to shoot up my house and my guests, so we hunkered down here to ascertain their intentions—before doing any shooting."

"Now comes the good part, I hope," Ed said.

"They approached my dock and, using my night binoculars . . . Hang on." He rummaged around in the cockpit before coming up with them. "In good working order. And using these, I was able to identify the two people aboard as Eben and Enos Stone—though I wasn't sure which was which. I handed Dino the glasses." He did so. "And Dino confirmed my judgment."

"Have they killed us yet?" Dino asked. "They've certainly had the time."

"Then they began firing. We ducked, in the hope they would stop, but they didn't, so we returned fire. That is, you returned fire, Ed. You're the one with the nightscope."

"Good by me. Now shut up and listen."

They listened and heard engine noises in the distance.

"Running fast," Ed said.

"Too fast for in the dark," Dino agreed.

As if they had taken Dino's advice, the power out there was reduced, and they came into the harbor more slowly.

"You just let me know when you've got a positive ID," Ed said. "I'll take it from there."

Everybody rammed in magazines and worked their slides.

"I hope they didn't hear that," Ed said. "That was not an inviting sound."

"Good," Stone said. "We had hoped it would warn them off, but it didn't work."

The engines were reduced to idle and a dim form appeared at the outer edges of their vision.

"Hold your fire," Stone said. "I see a hull."

"We all see a hull," Dino replied. "But is it the right one? Does the boat have a name painted on the hull?"

"Yes," Ed said.

"What's the name?"

"I'm trying to remember."

Stone trained his night glasses on the hull. "Could it be *Argo*?"

"Yes! That's the name," Ed responded. "Is that a positive ID?"

"Yes, but only of the boat," Stone said. "I can see a figure at the helm, slightly lit by the instrument panel lights. There's another figure standing in the cockpit, at the stern."

"They're less than a hundred yards out now," Ed said. "I can see the two guys through my scope."

"Can you identify either one?" Stone asked. "I figure we only have to ID one, since they're identical."

"Good point," Ed said, "but not yet."

"The one not driving just stood on something and is leaning on the cabin. Oh, shit."

"'Oh, shit' what?" Dino asked.

"Oh, shit, they've got a nightscope, too. I just saw the green flash."

Then the shooting started.

45

A round tore across Stone's left shoulder, and he hit the deck. They only got flesh, he thought, but a few inches lower and he would no longer have had a working heart.

"It's the twins!" Stone shouted. "Positive ID." He didn't actually have a positive ID, but whoever was out there was hostile enough to warrant shooting at.

Ed Rawls obliged. They were fifty yards out now, and he got a piece of somebody, who yelled, "OW!"

Dino's barrel was resting on the boat's gunwale, and he was firing short bursts, making his ammo last.

"You want some of this, Stone?" Rawls yelled.

"Yes!"

"Then get off your ass and return fire!"

Stone obliged, opting for short bursts like Dino. "Ed, are you finding anybody in that nightscope of yours?"

"They pop up like ducks in a shooting gallery," Ed said, "but they've been too quick for me. Hang on, I've got an idea."

"I'm glad *somebody* has an idea!" Dino shouted.

"Where's my canvas bag?" Ed demanded.

"I don't see your canvas bag," Stone said. "What's in it?"

"A surprise, if we're lucky."

"I hate surprises," Dino said.

"You'll like this one." Ed emptied his bag onto the deck and rummaged through the contents. They still had regular incoming rounds. "Got it!"

"What is it?" Stone asked.

"This will only work if they've got that explosive of mine on their boat." Ed held up a small radio and pulled out the antenna. "I rebuilt this, and I remembered the frequency."

"What are you waiting for?" Stone asked.

Ed held up the unit and pressed the button. The plastique exploded. Unfortunately, it didn't explode on the boat. The boom came from the southwest, across the island. Everybody turned and looked in that direction.

A fireball lit up the sky. During those few seconds, the Hinckley in the cove revved its three engines and tore out of there, toward the open bay.

Ed jumped out of the boat onto the dock. "Let's get over there and greet them when they get home!"

Everybody took their weapons and ran toward the house. Primmy saw them coming and opened the door. "What was that noise?" she asked.

"Something exploding on the other side of the island!" Stone shouted. "We're going over there and find out what. You stay here."

"Why do you get to have all the fun?" she yelled at his back as they ran through the living room and out the front door.

They took Ed's Range Rover, and he did the driving. They tore through the sleeping village and saw Billy Hotchkiss on the front porch of his store in an ankle-length nightshirt. "Hey!" he yelled as they drove past.

"Hey, yourself!" Dino called back.

Ed used his remote from a quarter mile away to open both his gates, and they roared down his driveway. They got out of the car and looked toward the twins' house. A chunk of one upstairs corner was missing, and there were little tongues of flame here and there.

"Shit, I wish I'd made it more incendiary!" Ed shouted. "Let's get down to the dock and give them a warm welcome!"

They ran down to the dock, where Ed's boat lay. "Hop in," Ed said. "This is a Hinckley, too, and it held up the last time they shot at it."

They leapt into the boat and looked at the next dock

down. "Shit!" Ed yelled. "They beat us back!" He snapped off a couple of rounds at two figures running across the newly laid parking area then up the front steps. "Those bastards must have been doing sixty knots in the dark to get back here that fast."

"I don't think we're going to get to kill them tonight," Dino said.

"I guess not," Ed said. "You guys want some ice cream? We got bourbon praline."

"Sure," Stone said.

They sat in the dark, eating ice cream and looking out the living room window at the twins running around, putting out fires.

"That's amusing," Dino said.

"Not as amusing as shooting them," Ed said, "but amusing."

The last of the flames at the house disappeared, finally. "Let's see if they still got any fight in them," Ed said. "If they do, they'll be over here in a minute."

"Interesting to speculate what it would have done to them if they'd been in their bed when that thing blew."

"You think they didn't find the bomb?"

"They must have found it, but were dumb enough to leave it in the room, thinking they'd disabled it. They'll be ordering new beds tomorrow, not to mention a new roof."

———

When Stone and Dino got home, everybody was sitting up, waiting, and they were all mad.

"What the hell?" Viv demanded.

"'What the hell,' what?" Dino countered.

"Where have you two been?"

"Over at Ed's eating ice cream."

"Oh, good," Viv said to Primmy and Carly. "They had ice cream."

"I'm happy for them," Primmy said. "Why did you have ice cream?"

"We were trying to beat them back to their house, but they got there first. The ice cream was an afterthought." He reached into a coat pocket. "But here's another pint for the three of you to share, courtesy of Ed Rawls. He wanted you to know where the credit lay."

"You tell Ed the credit is all his," Viv said, while Carly went for bowls and spoons.

Stone and Dino sat and watched the women eat their ice cream. When they had finished, Viv put down her bowl. "So, did you get the twins?"

"We think Ed nicked one of them," Stone said. "But they were both still able to run. Next time."

Viv sighed. "Next time. When is that going to be?"

"I don't know," Dino said. "But I've got to be in the office Monday morning, so it's probably going to be without me here to take the credit. Stone, do I need to order a plane?"

"No, I'll arrange for Faith to be here with the G-500 on Sunday morning. We'll meet them at Rockland."

"I hate leaving work undone," Dino said.

"I expect you'll have another shot at the twins," Primmy said, then refused to say more.

46

Billy Hotchkiss was driving out toward the point when he came to the Stone twins' place and stopped by the side of the road. "Just a minute," he said to the couple in his car. "I want to find out what happened." Billy felt a journalistic need to know everything, so he could report it to the island community.

One of the twins came down from upstairs to meet him.

"Morning, Billy," he said.

"Good morning, Enos," Billy replied, taking a stab.

"It's Eben," the twin said.

"Sorry."

"It's okay, everybody does it."

"What happened to your house?"

"A little accident with a gas camping stove," Eben said.

"It's new, and we were trying to light it. We were a little too successful."

"Much damage?"

"It'll be fixed by tonight," Eben said. "Tell everybody not to worry." Eben raised an arm to scratch his head, but winced and thought better of it.

"Shoulder pain?" Billy asked.

"A little; it comes and goes."

"Get some of that CBD cream. We've got some down at the store. It's good for pain like that."

"I'll do that. See ya, Billy." Eben turned and walked back into the house,

Billy returned to his customers. "Fella had an accident with a camping stove, one of those gas ones," he said to them. He drove them out to see the old house on the point. Then, on the way back, he pulled into the Jackson house, as it had come to be known on the island.

"I think this might be on the market soon," he said to them, "so I thought I'd give you an early look. The beauty of this place is that it's turnkey. It'll be for sale with all the furniture and fittings, down to the last spoon."

He took them through every room of the place, and they were impressed. They finished in the upstairs master suite.

"What's this going to list for?" the man asked.

"Probably three and a half million, furnished as you see

it. There's a barn and a boathouse and a dock out back, and it's all freshly renovated."

"Why would anybody put all this work and money into a property like this, then just walk away from it?" his wife asked.

"There was a tragedy, and they both died," Billy said. "The police said it was a murder/suicide."

The woman started to ask another question, but her husband raised a hand to stop her. "Don't ask," he said. "We don't want to know where it happened."

"I guess you're right," she said.

He pulled her aside, and they had a moment of earnest conversation. Finally, they rejoined Billy. "We'd like to make an offer," the husband said. "Three million."

"I don't think that's going to do it," Billy said, "not with all the furniture and everything. I know the owner, and he doesn't like to be lowballed."

"Three and a quarter?" the man asked.

Billy pointed upward with a thumb.

"Okay?" the man asked, misinterpreting the thumb.

Billy shook his head. "More."

"All right, three and a half, but that's as far as I'll go."

"All cash, or do you need a mortgage? I can help with that."

"All cash, a couple of weeks to close?"

Billy opened his notebook, took out an offer form and filled it in with lightning speed, then handed it to the man with a pen.

"It's owned by a corporation?" the man asked, looking over the form.

"The owner is a very private person. He doesn't want the transaction to make the papers, and frankly, neither do you. The summer folks here don't want outsiders to even know about the island, and especially not who's moving in and out."

"That's good for us," the man said. He signed the offer and handed it back to Billy. "When will we know?"

"Maybe today," Billy said.

"You mind if we just wander around for a few minutes?" the woman asked. "Pretend we own it?"

Billy smiled. "Sure. I'll sit out on the porch and make some calls." He went outside, took a rocker, and got out his cell phone.

Hello?"

"Stone, it's Billy. How are you?"

"Very well, Billy. You?"

"Me, too. I just had a word with Eben Stone, over at his house."

"Yeah? What did he have to say for himself?"

"He said they had an accident last night, trying to light a gas camping stove."

"Poor kids. Anybody hurt?"

"Eben was having a little shoulder pain."

"I wonder why?"

"Who knows. Listen, I have some good news for you."

"I always like to hear good news," Stone said.

"I was out, showing some prospective buyers around, and they expressed an interest in your place."

"This place?"

"No, the old Stone place. I walked them through, and they were impressed."

"How impressed?"

"Three and a half million impressed, as is. All cash, close in a couple of weeks. Does that impress you?"

"Not to tears, but I guess that would get me out from under."

"What do you say?"

"I say, call me late this afternoon."

"They're on the five o'clock ferry," Billy said. "Keep that in mind."

"I'll call you in an hour," Stone said, then hung up.

"What would get you out from under?" asked Dino, who had been listening.

"Billy got me an offer on the old Stone house. Three and a half million, furnished, as is."

"Sounds like a deal to me."

"How would you and Viv like to have a place up here?"

"We have such a nice place now, and the price is right." Dino said, waving an arm. "Why would we want to move?"

Stone called Billy back. "Sell it," he said.

"I'll bring the offer by for your signature; be there in a few minutes." He hung up.

Billy's customers were out back someplace. He put his feet up and gazed around him. The Stone house was across the way, a little uphill from where he sat. He could see the twins moving around their bedroom.

His customers appeared on the porch. "We're done," she said.

"You certainly are," Billy said. "Congratulations on your new house."

"We got it?"

"You did. I'll drop you off at the store, and I'll go get the offer signed."

"Who are those guys across the road?" the man asked.

"The brothers who are renovating the house."

"Are they twins?"

"Yep. Local characters." Billy was about to tell them more, but thought better of it. "Let's go," he said, and they left. He'd tell them more when they were used to the idea of owning their brand-new home.

47

The new owner of the Jackson place walked across the road while his wife poked around their new house. There was a young man sweeping the front porch, and there were various workmen doing things here and there.

"Good morning," the young man said.

"Good morning. My name is Smith Peterson. My wife, Coco, and I are going to be your neighbors across the road, and I thought I'd come and say hello."

"Well, congratulations," the young man said. "Come take a seat?"

Peterson walked up the steps and took a porch chair.

"I'm Eben Stone. My twin brother, Enos, lives here with me, but he's upstairs working on something."

"Don't bother him," Smith said. "There'll be plenty of time when we're moved in."

"Soon?"

"Couple of weeks."

"Where you folks from?"

"New York. I'm a dermatologist down there, but I'm beginning to take fewer patients these days. I reckon we'll be out of the city in a year."

"Well, you'll get a wonderful summer up here, and a terrible winter."

"Oh, we've got a place in Florida to take care of winter. Tell me, did I read something about you and your brother in the paper recently?"

"I expect so. Just about everybody did."

"What was it about?"

"Well, some years ago, we killed our abusive parents."

"I remember, now. You got a pardon, didn't you?"

"A lot of folks took up our cause, and we were vindicated, so we came back to the island where we spent our summers growing up. We teach criminal appeals at Yale Law two days a week in the summers."

"Was the house across the road where you grew up?"

"Yes, it was. We tried to buy it when we were released, but somebody outbid us."

"Look, Eben, we don't want there to be any hard feelings between us about our buying the house. If you and your brother still want it, we'll withdraw our offer and look elsewhere for a place."

"Well, that's very kind of you, Smith. But I speak for my brother, too, when I say that we're very happy in our new house, and we hope you'll be just as happy in yours."

"Thank you, Eben," he said. "I'd better run. I see my wife coming." He left and met his wife at their car. Eben Stone gave them a cheery wave as they drove away.

Stone went to the front door, let Billy Hotchkiss in, and waved him to a seat on the sofa.

"I've got the offer right here," Billy said, handing Stone a folder.

Stone opened and read it. "Smith Peterson and his wife, Coco," he said. "New York."

"That's right. He's a dermatologist and plastic surgeon. What is it they say about dermatologists?"

"Their patients never die, and they never get well," Stone said.

"That's right. The Petersons can afford it."

"Billy, how much have you told them about the provenance of the house?"

"You mean, about the twins?"

"And their connection to the house."

"Well, they've got their own place now," Billy said.

"They had their own place when they murdered the

Jacksons," Stone said. "Don't you get the feeling that they don't want anybody living there?"

"How much do you want me to tell them? What we know, or what we suspect?"

"Where are the Petersons now?"

"Over at the store, waiting for your signed acceptance."

Stone looked at his watch: 3:30. "Call them and invite them over here for a drink."

Billy rolled his eyes. "You're going to ditch this sale."

"Maybe not, but they'll go into the deal with their eyes open."

Billy reluctantly dug out his phone and called a number. "Mr. Peterson? Billy Hotchkiss. I'm over at the owner's place, a short way from the store. He'd like to meet you folks. Can you pop over here? Good." He gave them directions and hung up. "How are you going to approach this, Stone?" he asked.

"I don't know. We'll see."

Shortly, the bell rang, and Stone let in the Petersons and introduced himself. "Got time for a drink?" he asked.

"Always," Peterson said.

Stone sat them down and took care of that.

"We love the house and the way you've done it up," Smith said.

"Doing it up was the work of Billy's wife," Stone replied.

"She did a wonderful job."

"I'll tell her you said so," Billy said.

[251]

"Smith," Stone said. "Do you know anything about the provenance of the house you're buying?"

"Are you referring to the Stone twins?"

"I am."

"Yes, I read about it in the papers, and I met one of the twins, Eben, a few minutes ago."

"Oh? How did that come about?"

"I saw him sweeping his front porch, and I walked across the road and introduced myself. We had a nice chat."

"About the house?"

"That and their previous legal problems. He told me they had grown up in the house and had tried to buy it without success. I offered to withdraw my offer to allow them to buy it, if they still wanted to, but he said they were very happy in their place and would have no hard feelings about our buying it. That's about it."

"Did Eben mention that they were suspects in other crimes, murders, and kidnapping?"

"I read about that in the papers at the time. Insufficient evidence, I believe."

"That's correct, but it doesn't mean they're innocent."

Peterson shrugged. "It doesn't mean they're guilty, either."

"And this was all friendly?"

"Very friendly. I didn't meet his brother, who was upstairs working on some job or other."

"Smith, if you're at all uncertain about the house and

your new neighbors, I'd be happy for you to withdraw your offer."

"No, Stone, we won't do that. I'll hold you to your verbal acceptance."

Stone opened the folder and signed both copies of the offer. He kept one and gave the other to Peterson. "There you are," he said. "We'll look forward to seeing you sometime, after you've moved in. We'll be going back to New York in a few days, but we'll get back later in the summer."

The Petersons tossed off their drinks, shook hands, and left, tailed by Billy, who was looking very relieved.

48

Ed Rawls waited until well after dark, then took his rifle with the nightscope out of the house and across the road. He let himself into the old Stone house with a key that Primmy had given him and, without turning on any lights, walked upstairs to the master bedroom and looked out the front windows.

Across the road and up a bit he could see the twins' bedroom, with its lights all on. The boys were pulling mattresses out of boxes and laying them onto the electric bed frames. They carried the old, charred frames and the old mattresses down to the floor below and piled them in the parking area near the front steps for trash pickup the next day.

Ed took the opportunity to sight in on various spots in their bedroom, dry-firing on each. Finally, the twins came back upstairs with arms full of linens and made their beds. He could have killed them both in a few seconds, but then he wouldn't have an alibi.

Ed walked back downstairs and around the front yard, which was bordered by an old, chest-high boxwood hedge, probably planted by the twins' grandmother. Finally, he went back inside and walked up two flights to a guest bedroom, over the master suite. There was no porch up here, but each of the two windows offered ideal perches for him, level with the twins' bedroom. This would be his spot.

He went back downstairs and, after careful observation, trotted across the road, then walked back to his house.

"How'd it go, sweetie?" Sally asked.

"Couldn't have gone better. They'll wake up dead on Monday morning."

"Perfect."

"Perfect is good enough for me," Ed said.

Stone, Primmy, and Carly sat up with their cognac and waved Dino and Viv off to bed.

"I was surprised," Primmy said.

"At what?"

"That you didn't try to talk the Petersons out of buying your house."

"I thought I offered full disclosure," Stone said.

"Legally, maybe, but morally? Shouldn't you have told

them about your certainty that the twins did everything they were suspected of?"

"They were not in a mood to hear that," Stone said.

"Nevertheless . . ."

"Smith had had some doubts, I think, but his chat with Eben resolved them."

"He bought everything Eden said?"

"Why not? Eben's a charming young man who is thought to be innocent by half the people who know about him. He and Enos have been pardoned by the governor and had charges lifted a second time by the D.A. He was wholly convincing, Smith felt. And his wife looked as though she was accustomed to going along with his decisions on just about everything. It would have been churlish of me to deny them the house because of my own feelings."

"As long as you feel you've done the right thing, I won't worry about it anymore."

Carly, who had been silent through all this, spoke up, "If there were a guillotine available for use, I would be happy to pull the lever."

Stone laughed. "So everybody's on board?"

"Oh," Primmy said, "we've all been on board since the seaborne attack."

"So, you're both okay with finding a way to kill them?"

"I wouldn't pull the trigger," Primmy said, "but I wouldn't have a problem watching it done."

Stone laughed again. "I wouldn't like to be judged by a jury that had you both as members."

"If that should ever happen," Primmy said, "please remember to be innocent."

Finally, everyone went up to bed, except Stone, who poured himself a last, small brandy. He ran once more through the situation and its possible resolution. The Stone twins had put themselves in this situation, he reasoned. And the law, with all its power, had failed to make them accountable for their actions. They had painted Stone, as well as themselves, into a corner from which there were two ways out, and Stone had ruled out dying himself. That left the twins.

He tossed off the last sip of his brandy and went upstairs into the arms of Primmy.

49

Stone and Dino were enjoying a second cup of coffee the following morning, while the women were taking the sun on the dock, when the doorbell rang. Stone carefully used the peephole, then opened it. "Come in, Billy."

Billy entered looking troubled.

"Coffee?" Stone asked.

"Sure, black, please."

Stone poured a mug and handed it to him. "What's on your mind?"

"Your house," Billy said.

"Okay, which house?"

"The one you're selling to the Petersons."

"What troubles you about it?"

"The Petersons."

"You think they haven't got the cash to close?"

"Sure they have. You think I wouldn't check that out on a sale this size?"

"Then what about the Petersons?"

"I don't know."

Dino spoke up. "Does the deal smell bad, Billy?"

"No, the Petersons."

"Fishy smell?"

"No, there's a cop expression when something's not quite right about somebody."

"What's the expression?" Dino asked.

"That's what I'm asking you. You're the cop."

Dino stared at the ceiling. "Hinky?"

"That's it. There's something hinky about them."

"Dino," Stone said, "can you run their names?"

"What are their first names again?"

"Smith and Coco."

"Is Coco short for something?"

"Beats me. Nobody's named Coconut. Can you run their names?"

Dino got out his iPhone and went to work with his thumbs.

"One thing," Billy said, "is that they were both armed."

"With what?"

"Pistols. He was wearing a shoulder holster under his left arm, and I got a look into her bag, and there was a little, pearl-handled job in there."

"They're New Yorkers, right?"

Dino broke in. "Right, they are. And they're clean—not even an old parking ticket."

"See if they have carry licenses," Stone said.

Dino typed some more.

"Carry licenses are very difficult to get in New York," Stone explained to Billy.

"Yes," Dino said. "He does, not she. And it's only a few weeks old."

"Can you get a look at their application?" Stone asked.

"That will take a little longer," Dino said "Some more coffee might help."

Stone poured him more.

"Got it," Dino said.

"What did he give as a reason?"

"Says he has a crazy patient who has repeatedly threatened his life."

"I've never heard of a dermatologist with a murderous patient," Dino said.

"Who has?"

"Something else. His application includes a letter of recommendation from my chief of detectives. That's why he got the license." He dialed a number. "Hey, it's Dino. Is he in?" He listened. "Okay, do you know if he knows a dermatologist named Smith Peterson?" He listened. "Thanks, Christine." Dino hung up. "He's up the Amazon on a cruise ship, but his secretary says that Peterson is a friend from college days."

Stone looked at Billy. "He's got a crazy patient, and he knows the chief of detectives. You see anything hinky in that?"

Billy shook his head. "Nah, it's just a feeling, and I can't shake it."

"Are the Petersons still on the island?"

"I don't know. They were staying at the inn."

"Why don't you arrange to bump into them somewhere and put your nose back to work? Call me, if you learn something."

Billy finished his coffee and left.

"Maybe Billy is crazy," Dino said.

"I've never thought so, but he's very good at reading people."

"A valuable skill in a real estate guy."

"He told me once that he could always separate the lookers from the buyers," Stone said. "Right away."

"Apparently, he can separate the hinky from the normal, too," Dino said. "He just doesn't know why."

50

Billy found the Petersons where he expected them to be—where he, himself, would be if he had just bought an expensive property. They were on that property, walking around the exterior of the house.

"Good morning, Billy," Smith said.

"Morning, Smith. Morning, Coco."

"We were just having another look around, seeing if we missed anything."

"And did you?"

"Well, there's the Jacksons' car, the Mercedes station wagon. I phoned the lawyer whose number you gave me, and we made a deal. I'm sending him a check, and he's sending me the title."

"Excellent."

"Billy, do you have a key to the house with you?"

"I believe I do. Let me look." Billy went to his car, opened the center console, and found the key, properly tagged. "Come on, I'll let you in."

"We're going to be a while, I think," Smith said. "Do you mind if we keep the key?"

"I guess that's all right," Billy said. He walked back to his car, passing the Petersons' rental car. He hadn't noticed it before, but there was a leather pouch for a long weapon, a rifle or a shotgun, on the rear parcel shelf. He wondered how they traveled with that.

Smith came out on the upstairs porch and looked around.

"Oh, Smith," Billy called. "How did you folks travel here?"

"We have some friends who have a King Air they keep in New Jersey. Their pilot flew us directly to the island, where we called for a rental car."

"Will they come and get you when you leave?"

"Probably. We haven't thought that far ahead."

Billy gave them a wave and drove away in his car. Easy to bring a weapon on a private plane, he thought. Still, Peterson hadn't mentioned any intention to do some hunting, and that wasn't allowed on the island, anyway.

He got back to the store, then retrieved the Petersons' file. Time to put the closing package together. Some of the papers had gotten combined with the Jacksons' file, and he sorted them out. As he did, something caught his eye, something in the brokerage agreement they had signed.

Grace Jackson had filled out their information sheet and signed the brokerage agreement. She had signed it Grace P. Jackson. He sat down at his computer and entered Grace P. Jackson obituary into the search bar. One came up immediately, the kind submitted by the funeral home. Grace's maiden name was Peterson, and her only sibling was a brother, Smith Ames Peterson, MD. Billy printed the obit and took it with him.

He drove over to Stone Barrington's house and rang the bell. "I know," he said when Stone opened the door, "you're seeing too much of me."

"Not at all, Billy. Come right in."

Stone could see that Billy had found something. He was practically bursting to tell him.

Dino came into the room and joined them.

"What is it, Billy?"

"I found out a little more about the Petersons," he said. "Look at this obituary."

Dino stood behind Stone, and they both read the obit.

"Grace's maiden name was Peterson?"

Billy nodded. "And she had one sibling: Smith Peterson."

"And you consider this hinky?" Dino asked.

"A little out of the ordinary," Billy replied. Grace and Henry Lee Jackson pretend to buy the house for Stone, then they . . ."

"Were murdered," Stone said.

"Not too long after that, Grace's brother shows up, looks at two houses and buys yours immediately."

"Did he inquire about who lived across the road?"

"Not only did he inquire, but if you'll remember, he walked over there and introduced himself to Eben."

"And offered to withdraw from the sale, if the twins still wanted it?"

"Right. Oh, and something else. The Petersons traveled here in a friend's King Air, directly to our airfield."

"What's hinky about that?" Dino asked.

"He brought a long weapon with him. It's on the parcel shelf of his rental car. I'm sure you know, Stone, that the shooting of firearms is prohibited on the island. Indeed, anywhere in Maine except hunting areas and only with a hunting license. Nobody hunts on the island."

"Rifle or shotgun?"

"Couldn't tell; it was in a leather pouch."

"That smell wasn't fish, Dino," Stone said. "Maybe it was revenge."

"What should we do about that?" Dino asked.

"We should get out of Smith Peterson's way," Stone replied.

Billy lifted his hands, as if in surrender. "I was never part of this conversation," he said, taking the documents from Stone, "and I don't remember anything said. Good day, gentlemen." Billy fled the house.

51

Stone and Dino got into the MG and drove down to Ed Rawls's house. They were admitted through the gates.

Ed was sitting on his front porch, working on the *Times* crossword. "Gents," he said.

"May we have a word, Ed?"

Ed looked at them suspiciously, but waved them to chairs. "Is this trouble?"

"Not necessarily," Stone said. "It's just that some new information has come to light, which might affect our actions."

"That doesn't sound good."

"We may have some competition in dealing with the twins."

"Competition? On the island?"

"Recently arrived," Stone replied.

"How recently?"

"Very. Now stop asking questions, and let me explain. Then you can ask questions."

"Promise?"

"Shut up and listen, Ed." Stone explained about the new buyers of his house and Billy's research.

"So, you're telling me that these people paid three and a half mil for your house, just to get a shot at the twins?"

"Not entirely. I think they may have heard about the house from the Jacksons and got interested. On the other hand, I think they knew that having the house would give them an opportunity to take a shot at the boys, while giving them a legit reason to be on the island. Who would believe they bought an expensive house merely to use it as a shooting platform?"

"Okay," Ed said, "let's assume that you're not entirely crazy and that this guy, Peterson, is fairly sane, too."

"Agreed on both accounts."

"What do you want me to do about it?"

"I was hoping you might have a suggestion," Stone said.

"Well, I've been working on this for some time now, and I'm attracted to the idea of ending the twins' time on the planet. So why don't you just tell Dr. Peterson to fuck off?"

"It would be rude to say that to a man who's giving me three point five million," Stone said.

"Are you saying that if I kill the twins before Peterson

gives you the money, he might just drive off into the sunset, leaving you holding the real estate?"

"I hadn't thought of it that way, but now that you mention it . . . That would be a consideration."

"Well, if we wait until after Peterson hands you the cash, he would take possession right away, wouldn't he?"

"I expect so."

"Then that would rob us—and by 'us,' I mean me—of the ideal shooting platform, wouldn't it?"

"I suppose that's true."

"Of course, we could just leave the good doctor to clean up the situation for us, right?"

"Maybe."

"'Maybe' is what I think, too. You know, dermatology is not, as I recall, one of the martial arts."

"It is not."

"So what if he misses? Or worse, what if he hits one twin, but not both?"

"Not desirable," Stone admitted.

"Do we have any information on whether Dr. Peterson has ever squeezed the trigger of a loaded weapon?"

"We do not."

"Or whether he has served in the military?"

"Not that, either."

"If he has served in the military, and if we could somehow come across his service record, then we might learn how he fared on the rifle range."

"I wouldn't know how to access a man's service record," Stone said.

"I would," Dino interjected. "But I'd have to go through channels, and in doing so would leave fingerprints."

"Do you have any other biographical information that might help me pick him out of a lineup of a great many other Petersons?" Ed asked.

Stone thought about that. "His middle name is Ames. Betcha there aren't too many Smith Ames Petersons."

"It's worth a stab," Ed said. "Let me go rub my computer's belly and see if it will cough up something to guide us." Rawls left them.

"Okay," Dino said when he had gone. "Suppose Ed comes up with a service record that says the guy can fire a rifle without shooting himself in the foot? What then?"

"I haven't the foggiest," Stone said.

52

Stone and Dino had been admiring the view for a quarter of an hour before Ed returned and dragged up his chair and shuffled through some papers he held in his hand.

"Well?" Stone asked after a while.

"Well . . . This Peterson is quite a fella."

"We're not looking for a character reference," Stone said.

"Well, if you were, you'd get a glowing one."

"From whom?"

"From near 'bout everybody who's ever met him."

"All right, Ed," Stone said, trying not to sound exasperated, "tell me about the charms of Smith Peterson."

"Academically, first in his high school, college, and med school classes. How's that for a start?"

"Just swell. Can he shoot people dead without fainting?"

Ed held up a finger. "There's more."

"Okay, what else?"

"You know what he did when he got out of med school?"

"Did a dermatology residency, I imagine."

"After that."

"Was a missionary in the Amazon?"

"Next best thing: he joined the Marines."

"Oh. You mean, he's mentally unbalanced."

"There was a war in Iraq, I think it was, and he thought it was his duty to serve."

"Ah, a patriot."

"I hope I didn't hear a smirk in that description," Ed said.

"You did not. It was sincere and heartfelt. Somehow, however, I think there's more to this story, if I can pry it out of you."

"Did I mention that his high school offered ROTC?"

"You did not."

"And that he volunteered for it?"

"Go on. Please."

"And that he was the best shot in his school? Same in college."

"Wait a minute, he would have gotten an ROTC commission."

"You're right, but he wouldn't take it. Instead, he joined the Marines as an ordinary enlistee. In his weapons training, he fired Expert in every weapon they threw at him."

"Finally, we get somewhere."

"He was snatched up and trained as a sniper."

"Oh, boy!"

"He got a battlefield commission, due to his high intelligence and superior intellect. Did I mention his leadership qualities?"

"No need," Stone said. "Goes without saying."

"When his enlistment was up, he declined to reenlist, in spite of entreaties and promises of an eventual star or two on his shoulder, and guess what he did then?"

"I give up."

"He became a dermatologist and excelled at it, opened his own practice with a partner, and got rich."

"Every dermatologist's dream, I would imagine."

"Who cares? Point is, he's highly qualified for the position he came here to fill, and he may be nearly as good a shot as I am."

"So, are we going to encourage him or discourage him?"

"Discourage him," Ed said firmly.

"Why?"

"Because all the shooting skills in the world don't prepare a man to be a murderer."

"Surely, he would have murdered many people in Iraq."

Ed shook his head. "Those were kills, accomplished on orders from a chain of command. A man can be a killer, without being a murderer. Murder requires a different mindset. You, being an ex-cop, might call it a motive."

"Revenge is a pretty good motive."

"That doesn't mean he can act on it with impunity."

"I see, I think."

"And it especially doesn't mean he can get away with it. Billy Hotchkiss, you, and I all tracked him down in a matter of a couple of hours. How long do you think it would take the real police?"

"You have a point."

"He certainly does," Dino said.

"And all that academic and military training—all that financial success—will be for naught. He'll spend the rest of his days in prison."

"And yet, the Stone twins are walking around, free as the air they breathe."

"Yeah, but they're insane; Smith Peterson is as sane as you or I, maybe saner."

"So what are we going to do about it?"

"There's no 'we' in this, just you. You're going to have to have a chat with Smith Peterson and talk him down."

53

When Stone got home he called Billy Hotchkiss.

"Hey, Stone."

"Billy, do you know if Smith Peterson is on the island right now?"

"No, but I can call him for you."

"Would you ask him to come and see me at the earliest possible moment?"

"Sure. See you later." Billy hung up.

Ten minutes later, the phone rang. "Hello?"

"Stone, it's Smith Peterson."

"Hi, Smith. Are you on the island?"

"Yes, we're at the inn. We're about to go over to the house and measure some things."

"Could I meet you there? There's something I'd like to discuss with you."

"Sure. We'll be there in a quarter of an hour. See you then." He hung up.

Stone was approaching the house when he saw the Petersons pull into the driveway ahead of him. He got out and strolled over to the porch. Coco went inside, and Smith pointed to a chair. "Have a seat."

Stone sat down. "I see you've got a long gun in your car."

"A Remington deer rifle, thirty-ought six."

"I don't know if you're aware that hunting is prohibited on the island."

"I do know now, but I didn't when I was deciding to bring the rifle. I expect I can find somewhere on the mainland that I could bag a buck."

"I'd recommend a place, if I knew one."

"Don't worry about it."

"Smith, you and I need to have an intimate chat, one more personal than either of us might be comfortable with."

Smith's brow wrinkled. "Okay, what's on your mind?"

"You are the brother of a former occupant of this home, Grace Jackson, who was murdered here along with her husband."

Smith did not reply.

"Do you know what Henry Lee Jackson did for a living?"

"He was a civil servant of some sort, I believe."

"Does your knowledge of him go any further than that? He was, after all, your brother-in-law."

Smith regarded Stone evenly. "Let's just say that Henry Lee and I were the closest of friends, as close as brothers, as close as I was to my sister, Grace."

"Then you're aware of where in the government they both worked."

"I am, I . . . Did you say 'both worked'?"

"I did."

"Now that, I did not know. I thought Grace was a housewife."

"No. Do you know the nature of the work Henry Lee and Grace did?"

"Not specifically. He gave me to understand that it was confidential."

"Do you know how much money Henry Lee earned?"

"Not exactly."

"Did you believe him to have the means to pay three and a half million dollars for a house?"

"I believe he had private means beyond a government salary."

"What reason do you have to believe that?"

"That's what he told me, when I asked him that question. I wanted to help, if I could, but he told me that would be unnecessary. Please tell me what you're getting at, Stone, and where you're getting your information."

"The Jacksons never owned this house. They were decoys, set up there by a certain government agency as a last job before retirement."

"I don't understand."

Stone handed him his Agency business card. "I'm in a position to get a lot of information about a lot of people," he said. "You, for instance."

"What do you know about me?"

"Just about everything," Stone said. "And what I don't know, I can pretty accurately guess."

Smith sat back in his chair and gazed at Stone. "Go ahead, tell me what you want to know, and I'll help, if I can."

"I know about your military record and your shooting skills, and I can guess how you want to employ those skills. Do you think you're up to that?"

"I do. I think that, if you know so much about me, you must know that I shot and killed seventy-one men and three women when I was in the military."

"I do. Do you consider that you murdered them?"

"Certainly not. I killed them in the line of duty."

"Do you know the difference between line of duty and murder?"

"Murder is an illegal act, and an immoral one."

"Very good distinction."

"Are you a priest or clergyman of some sort?"

"Hardly. I'm an attorney and a former police officer. And I'm here to try and help you understand that murder, in addition to being illegal and immoral, is a very dangerous act—to the murderer. I don't suppose that during your training, anyone explained that to you."

"It wasn't necessary. I knew that I could be killed."

"But you didn't fear arrest, trial, conviction, or punishment."

"Of course not."

"Those are the things you have to fear now. You have a great deal to lose, not excepting your life."

"Perhaps you'd better tell me what you believe I intend to do."

"I believe you're going to try to murder the Stone twins, and that your motive is revenge for the death of your brother-in-law and closest friend, and your sister."

"Do you also believe that I intend to be caught?"

"No, but nevertheless you will be. You have been trained as an assassin, but not as a suspect or a fugitive. It took me and my friends only a couple of phone calls and a laptop computer to figure that out. How long do you think it would take the Maine State Police? I have dealt with the local representatives of that body, and they are neither stupid nor without resources."

"They've had every opportunity to catch the Stones, but they haven't done so. Nor have they been able to keep them in prison, after being sentenced."

"They did catch and convict the Stones, even if their efforts were later overridden. It helped that their father was close to the governor when they were in college. Is your father close to the governor?"

"My father is dead."

"I'm sorry for your loss. What do you think he would advise you, if he were still alive?"

Smith looked away for the first time. "That is irrelevant."

"The way he brought you up is not irrelevant. Did he teach you that, if you committed a crime you would be caught and punished?"

"Of course."

"Do you think he was lying to you?"

"No."

"But now, your hatred of your friend's murderers has been sufficient to cause you to ignore his teaching. Let me tell you, hatred and revenge are very difficult motives to conceal. If I were examining you under oath, it would take me only a couple of minutes to establish your hatred of the twins. Conviction for murder requires motive, means, and opportunity. Also, bad luck helps. You have all of that in abundance."

"What about 'beyond a reasonable doubt'?"

"That will be wrapped up in the first three."

Smith said nothing.

"Are you aware that the twins are extremely dangerous? Isn't that why you sought to disarm them by offering them the opportunity to buy the house? You may be sure that they saw through that and they know who you are. They likely view you and Coco as replacements for Henry Lee and Grace. It is very unlikely that you would survive an attempt to kill them. Even if you did, it is even less likely that you would remain a free man. Think what that would mean to your wife. Even if she avoids conviction as an accessory, is she supposed to spend the rest of her life visiting you once a week and bringing you cakes with files baked into them?"

A very long pause. "You have a point," Smith said.

"Thank you. Perhaps it would help to restrain your ardor if I told you that others—as well-trained and proficient as you—are interested in seeing the twins brought to justice."

"Is that so?" Smith asked earnestly.

Stone nodded. "And they are much more likely to achieve that result without danger to themselves."

"Who are these people?"

"They are better friends than you know, or need to know." Stone stood up. "If you want to survive this episode in your life, it's better that you start now. How did you travel here?"

"A friend in New York has a King Air. His pilot flew us directly to the island."

"Can you recall the airplane?"

"Yes, if it's not in use."

"You should do so now. Do you have any clothing or personal effects at the inn?"

"No, we checked out a little while ago. We had planned to sleep here tonight."

"Call about the airplane."

Smith produced a phone and made the call, then hung up. "The airplane is in the air, returning to Teterboro from the Hamptons. They can divert and be here in an hour. I'd better explain things to Coco."

"You can do that when you reach the airfield," Stone said. "Let's not waste any more time here."

They locked the house and loaded their things, while Stone kept a watchful eye on the twins' house.

Stone followed them to the airfield and waited with them, watching the perimeter. The King Air was late by ten minutes, but the pilot had no problem with the short field length. Stone helped them load their belongings.

"Listen," Smith said, "we still want to close on the house. Once all this is cleared up, we can move in."

"I'll let you know when it's safe," Stone said.

They shook hands, then boarded the airplane. Five minutes later the pilot set the flaps for takeoff, revved the engines to full throttle, then, after a moment, released the brakes. The aircraft used all the runway, then lifted off and turned south.

Stone felt vastly relieved. He drove slowly back to his house and arrived to find Dino and Viv sitting in the living room, reading.

"Where are Primmy and Carly?" he asked.

"They left a few minutes ago," Viv said.

"Left for where?"

"They didn't say, but they took bathing suits with them."

Outside, the skies darkened, and it began to rain. They could hear thunder in the distance, growing closer, and the rain became dense. The lights in the house went out, then came back on a few seconds later, as the generator kicked in.

"Not a good day for a swim," Stone said.

"Thunderstorms don't last long," Viv said. Then, as if to confirm her judgment, the lights dimmed again, then came back bright, as the generator turned itself off. A moment later, the sun was shining again.

"Now," Dino said quietly to Stone, "all we have to do is make sure the twins don't kill us before Ed can kill them."

54

Stone read for a while, then he went outside and looked at the skies. Cloudless. The sun was high. He went back inside and wondered where Primmy and Carly were. Finally, he got out his cell phone and called Primmy's number. The call went directly to voicemail. He left her a message to call him, then hung up.

"You have no idea where they are?" he asked the Bacchettis.

"I know nothing," Dino said, "just like you."

"Viv, do you know where Primmy and Carly are?"

Viv ignored him. "Viv, can you hear me now?" Stone asked, raising his voice.

Viv lifted a finger to her lips for silence, then ignored him again.

Stone tried Primmy again: nothing.

Dino leaned over and said softly, "Try Ed Rawls. They could be with him."

Stone called Rawls; no reply. "It's as though everyone has gone on radio silence," he said.

The phone rang, the landline. Stone picked it up, expecting to hear Primmy's voice. "Hello?"

"Stone, it's Billy. I just got a call from the mainland. Lightning struck the cell tower above Lincolnville, and service is out."

"How long?" Stone asked.

"No one seems to know."

"Thanks, Billy. Have you seen Primmy and Carly this afternoon?"

"Nope. It's been pretty quiet around here. The rain drove everybody indoors."

"Thanks, Billy," Stone said, then hung up.

"What does Billy have to say for himself?" Dino asked.

"He says lightning struck the cell tower over at Lincolnville, and our service is out. Nobody knows how long."

"Good," Viv said.

"What?" Dino asked.

"Sometimes, a lack of cell service is a good thing," she said. "It reminds us of the good old days."

"You mean the good old days of the landline?"

Stone picked up the phone to call Ed Rawls on his landline, then he remembered Rawls had no landline. He had been one of the first to go all cell.

He looked up Primmy's landline number in the local directory and picked up the phone. It was dead. "So much for the good old days of the landline," he said. "Now it's out, too."

"Shush," Viv said. "Try the good old days of reading a book. They work, even when the phones don't."

"Annoying, isn't she?" Dino asked.

55

Stone finally couldn't stand it anymore. Primmy and Carly were gone and unreachable. Ed Rawls couldn't be phoned. And Viv wasn't speaking to him.

"Dino," he said finally, "I'm going to take a look around the island. You want to come along?"

Dino opened his mouth to speak, but Viv spoke first. "Dino," she said, "I'd feel safer if you would stay here with me."

There must have been something in her voice that Dino could hear, but he was deaf to, Stone decided. "Oh, the hell with them," Stone muttered to himself.

"What was that you said?" Viv asked.

"Never mind, I was just talking to myself."

"Why don't you just calm down, sit down, and read a book."

"Dino," Stone said. "Do you have any idea what's going on here?"

Dino looked at him dolefully, then put a finger to his lips.

Stone got his shoulder holster and pistol from Dick Stone's little office, put them on and grabbed some ammunition magazines, and shoved them into his bush jacket pocket. He struggled into that and walked across the living room toward the front door. "Good afternoon to you," he said putting on a straw hat to keep the sun off.

"Bye," Viv replied. Dino said nothing, apparently having been switched off by Viv.

Stone walked into the garage and found it empty. He remembered that Seth had gone into Camden for something and had taken the station wagon, but the MG was gone, too. Primmy's car was apparently at her house, so he was stranded.

Then Stone remembered that he had legs and that there were feet attached to them. He started walking.

It took him twenty minutes to get to the village and the store. He looked inside and saw Billy seated at his desk, as usual; otherwise, the store was empty.

"Hey, Stone," Billy said.

"Any word on the cell service?"

"I got a call on the landline saying that the repairmen were on the way from Augusta, then the landline went down. I don't know why."

"Will you do me a favor, Billy?"

"Sure."

"Call me on my cell when the service is restored?"

"Sure, glad to, Stone."

Stone continued up the road toward Ed Rawls's house.

A few minutes earlier, Sally had come out onto the porch where Ed Rawls was reading the papers. "The girls are on the move," she said.

"Okay, thanks." Ed got up, went inside, got into his shooting vest, and stuffed magazines into his pockets. He mounted the scope to his rifle and attached a shoulder strap, then he went into a closet and got out the pair of strap-on lineman's blades, slung the rifle over his shoulder, and took his binoculars to the window and surveyed the twins' property. All was quiet, and so was the Jackson property.

"Ed, I don't often say this to you," Sally said, "but you need to be extra careful today. It's going to be dangerous out there."

"I know it," Ed said. He put on his floppy, cotton khaki hunting hat and let himself out the door facing the dock. He turned right and went around the side of the house facing away from the twins' place, then walked to the back corner. He took out a hand mirror from one of the vest's many pockets and held it around the corner, getting a fix on the upstairs wraparound porch, and watched for signs of movement. Nothing.

A cross the road, in the Jackson house, Primmy and Carly sat silently in the upstairs bedroom. Primmy looked at her watch. "It's time," she said.

"Okay," Carly replied, getting to her feet.

"Any second thoughts?" Primmy asked.

"I don't think so," Carly said. "I'm committed."

"Me, too,"

The girls leaned Primmy's shotgun against the doorjamb, along with their handguns, then walked out onto the upstairs front porch. "Don't look at the twins' house," Primmy said, "not even for a second."

"Right," Carly replied.

"Ready?"

"Ready," Carly replied.

"Slowly," Primmy said. "There's no hurry."

The two women began removing their clothing.

R awls checked his wristwatch, then got onto his belly and began crawling through the high grass behind his house. On his elbows and knees, he worked his way slowly to the side of the road. He looked across at the Jackson house and couldn't believe what he was seeing, but he knew it was real, so he kept at it. He used his binoculars to survey the twins' house, then stood up into a crouch, then ran across the road and dived into the grass on the other side. He crawled a few more feet to a large tree, then got behind it before he could be seen.

Ed was momentarily transfixed by the sight of the two women on the upper porch, stark naked and, apparently, doing stretching exercises.

Ed took a long strap from a pocket, handed it around the tree, fastened it to his belt, and started climbing the tree, using his gloved hands and the barbs strapped to his ankles.

Stone trudged on up the road toward Rawls's house. Then he came around a corner and caught a glimpse of what appeared to be naked flesh on the upstairs porch of the Jackson house. He wasn't sure what he was seeing, so he ran across the road and continued slowly toward the house. A little winded from his exertions, Stone leaned against a tree and mopped his brow with his handkerchief. Then he heard a voice.

"Stone, don't move. Freeze right there!" said the voice in a loud whisper.

It took Stone a moment to realize that the voice was Rawls's. "Ed?" he whispered back.

"Shut up, and stay on the side of the tree away from the twins' house."

Stone froze for a moment. "Where are you?" he whispered.

"In a deer blind," Rawls whispered back. "In the tree above your head."

Stone looked up. "What are the girls doing on that porch?" Stone asked.

"Sun bathing," Rawls said. "Now shut up, or they'll hear you and ruin everything."

56

Eben Stone stood on a ladder in the master bedroom of their house, securing the mount for a ceiling light fixture, while Enos held the ladder for him.

"Holy shit!" Enos said. "Do you see what I see?"

"Where?" Eben asked.

"Across the road."

Eben drove the screw home and attached the chain from the fixture to the beam, then he turned and looked across the road. "Holy shit!" he said.

The two of them watched, transfixed, while the women did slow-motion stretching exercises.

"They're just asking for it," Enos said.

"I believe you're right," Eben replied, sliding down the ladder to the floor. "Can they see us?"

"I think we're in shadow," Enos replied.

Eben walked quickly to the window, staying out of the women's sight line, and looked up and down the road. "One car there, Barrington's MG, but no sign of him or anybody else."

"I think we should visit them," Enos said.

"Maybe that's what they're hoping we'll do."

"Where are those plastic ties?"

"In a bag, just outside the door, in the hall," Eben said. "While you're at it, bring that tube of petroleum jelly from the bathroom."

Enos retrieved those items and put them into a tote bag.

"We'd better pack weapons, as well," Eben said, "in case they're reluctant."

"They don't look reluctant to me," Enos replied. "In fact, they look very welcoming."

"Let's see if we can get across the road without being seen," Eben said, "then we can come in the back way and give them a nice surprise."

"Good idea." Enos peeked up and down the road. "It's clear. If we leave through the back door, we can walk uphill about forty feet, then cross without their seeing us."

The two strapped on handguns, one grabbed the tote bag, and they went downstairs and out the rear door of the house.

Ed Rawls caught a glimpse of them as they crossed the road from his perch in the deer blind. "Heads up!" he whispered to Stone. "The boys are on the move." He sighted through the scope to be sure he had coverage of the whole porch. This was going to be a delicate shot, if he could pull it off, and if he couldn't, he was going to have to get a second shot off quickly.

"I want to come up there," Stone said.

"No, it won't support the weight of both of us. And anyway, one of us should cover the porch from the ground."

"Oh, all right," Stone said, "but I can't see anything from here."

"You're missing quite a show," Ed said. Then he heard a cracking noise—and what was more, felt it. "Oh, shit!" he muttered.

"What?" Stone quietly called back.

The twins crept up the back stairs of their old home, then stopped and listened for movement in the house. They both heard a faint cracking noise. They looked at each other and shrugged, then, on Eben's signal, they began making their way through the house to the front.

The women finished their exercises, then stretched out on a double-width folding cot.

"This clearly isn't working," Primmy said. "Is it time for phase two?"

"If that doesn't do it, then they're just not receptive," Carly replied. "I'm game for phase two, if you are."

The twins reached the master suite and tiptoed across the carpeted floor toward the windows. Eben held up a hand, then started to strip off his clothes and his weapon. Enos followed suit, then reached for the bag with the ties and the lubricant.

Here goes," Primmy said. She leaned over and kissed Carly on the lips. "Make some noise," she whispered.

Carly gave out a low moan, then Primmy kissed her on a nipple and bit lightly.

"Ahhhhhhh!" Carly cried. "More!"

Ed saw a curtain move inside the upper porch window and brought his rifle up. Doing his best to ignore the women's actions, he got ready for someone to step onto the porch.

Stone peeped around the tree, but saw little. Then he heard a louder cracking noise than before. After that, things seemed to happen in slow motion.

57

Stone started around the tree for a better angle.

Ed Rawls saw a naked twin step onto the porch, but his brother did not immediately follow. The twin clapped his hands, and a bag flew from inside the house into his hands. The women seemed to be so involved in their performance that they didn't notice. Then the second twin stepped outside, and Ed sighted them through the scope. Almost, he breathed. A little farther.

Then the limb gave way beneath the deer blind and Ed began falling. Stone got off a round before the limb struck him, but he had no idea if he'd hit anything. He took the limb across the back of his neck and went down and, for a few seconds, out.

———

The noise made Primmy look around, and the first thing she saw was a naked man holding a tube of something. "Carly, run!" she shouted.

"Run where?" Carly asked, sitting up. Then she saw the man, too, and a second man joined him. "Where the hell is Ed?"

They heard a great creaking sound as a branch snapped off a tree near the porch. The twins spun around and stared.

Primmy saw her chance and sprang for the door, landing on the floor, within reach of the shotgun. Carly was right behind her, grabbing her handgun. "Freeze!" Primmy yelled, in her best TV-show shout. The twins backed up against the porch railing and stared at them both. Then, as one man, they turned, grabbed the porch railing and vaulted over it into space.

The women ran to the railing, their weapons before them, and looked down. What they saw was a tangle of male bodies, two of them naked and bleeding, Stone looking shaken and dazed. Ed Rawls was struggling to get the twins off of him and to pry his rifle from under them.

"Freeze!" Primmy yelled again. But no one took any notice of her. She and Carly watched.

"We can't fire," Carly said. "Who's who?"

"The twins are naked," Primmy said, "that's all I know, but I don't have a shot."

Stone was able to sit up now, and was observing the scene as a stream of blood ran from his scalp, down his forehead, and into his eyes. He grappled for his handgun in its shoulder holster and got it out while wiping at his eyes with his free hand. Finally he could see a little. He looked up and saw two naked women standing on the porch, holding weapons. "Shoot somebody!" he shouted.

"Who?" Primmy shouted back.

"Somebody naked. You've got the angle!"

Primmy brought up the shotgun, racked the slide, pointed it down, then turned her head away, closed her eyes, and fired. The noise was horrific.

Ed was crawling away from the twins as fast as he could, dragging his rifle.

Stone could see out of one eye now. He raised his handgun to aim at something.

One of the twins stood, his back to a porch piling. He cupped his hands in front of him, making a stirrup, and shouted at his brother, "Up! Get the shotgun!"

Stone raised his gun and snapped off two shots in their general direction, then rubbed at his blocked eye. He had never been a great shot with a handgun, and he was going to need both eyes, if he wanted to hit something.

"Stone!" Rawls shouted. "Hold your fire! Hold your fire!"

Stone leaned against the tree and groped for a handkerchief.

"Don't shoot any more, anybody. You might hit me!" Ed shouted again. He was on his feet now and was aiming his rifle at the twins, who had collapsed into a heap at the foot of the piling.

Stone could see now. "Ed, don't finish them off!" he shouted.

"Why the hell not?" Rawls said, walking up to them with the rifle. "One each in the head will do it."

"Look at them, Ed. They're dead!"

"Dead my ass," Rawls replied. "They don't die that easy."

Stone walked over to the pile, holding his gun before him. "Then get a pulse."

Ed bent over and felt at the neck of one, then of the other.

"Jesus Christ," he said. "They're both dead, but how?"

Stone helped him and they pulled the twins apart. One had a bullet wound in his back at the base of his neck, the other a wound in the chest.

"How many shots did you fire?" Rawls asked.

"Two, I think, but I don't think one of them hit anything. I couldn't see very well."

"Give me a hand," Rawls said, taking an arm and hoisting.

Stone helped, and he and Rawls lifted the body. "There," Rawls said. "You killed them both with one round."

Rawls let the body go, took out his hunting knife and walked to the wooden support and dug into it with the blade. A moment later, he had a slug in his hand. "What are you firing?"

"Nine millimeter," Stone replied.

"See if the one with the slug in his chest has an exit wound."

Stone rolled him over. "No," he said.

"Well, at the shooting range, that shot would have won you a big, fuzzy, pink rabbit."

Then Primmy was standing next to Stone, still naked, dabbing at his scalp with a cloth soaked in vodka. "Here," she said, taking his empty hand and pressing it to his head, "hold that in place while I get another cloth."

Rawls shouted up at the porch. "Carly!" he yelled. "Throw me down a couple of blankets."

"Will beach towels do?"

"Yes!"

She dropped the towels over the railing, and Rawls began the job of wrapping up the bodies and securing them with duct tape from his bag.

"I saw some leaf bags in the barn," Rawls said to her. "Get me four of them, will you?"

Carly disappeared.

Primmy came back, wearing clothes now, with another

towel and some big Band-Aids and cleaned up Stone, while Ed and Carly got the bodies into the double leaf bags.

"There's not much cleaning up to do," Rawls said. "They both died instantly, so they didn't bleed much." He kicked dirt over what was on the ground.

"Stone, let's get these into your car and down to my boat," Rawls said. "The sun will be setting in half an hour. You ladies clean up the inside of the house and the porch. Tomorrow, I'll come by and patch that bullet hole in the porch support, and we'll be clear."

Stone and Rawls got the bagged corpses into the back of the MG and moved them over to Rawls's dock, where they loaded them into the boat.

"You're going to need some help dumping them," Stone said.

"No, I've got enough iron and chain around here to handle it. You make sure our crime scene is in order, and then get the girls home. I'll take care of everything here. Oh, and give me your gun."

Stone handed it to him. "Nice piece, but it has to go into the bay with the bodies."

"Thank you, Ed," Stone said.

"For what? You did all the shooting."

Back at Stone's house, everybody had a drink.

"Did everything go as planned?" Dino asked.

"No," Stone said, "but there was a happy ending. You knew about this, didn't you?"

"They made me promise not to tell you," Dino said. "They said if you knew, you wouldn't let them do it."

"It wasn't an entirely unhappy experience," Primmy said, and Carly laughed a lot.

58

The following morning, while the others were packing the Ford, Stone drove over to Ed Rawls's house. To his surprise, both gates stood open. Stone paused long enough to be identified on a monitor, then drove in and parked.

Ed and Sally were lazing on the front porch, sharing the *Times*. "Hey," Ed said.

"What's with the open gates?" Stone asked. "I've never seen that before."

"Today there is no threat," Rawls replied, then took a pencil from behind his ear and wrote something on the crossword.

"Have the packages been disposed of?" Stone asked.

Rawls lifted an eyebrow. "What packages?"

Stone nodded. "We're off to New York this morning,"

he said. "We're going to drop Carly at the New Haven airport to pick up her car and get packed, then she's driving to the city. She starts tomorrow morning at Woodman & Weld."

"They'll be lucky to have her, if they can stand her," Rawls said.

"Well, there is that."

"Can you get five people and their luggage off the ground in that Cessna?"

"Getting off the ground isn't the problem. It's getting off the ground before you run out of runway. That's solved by having only half fuel aboard."

"Right."

"The G-500 will meet us at Rockport." Stone sighed. "I wish I could say it's been fun, Ed, but it's been unusual. I'll give you that."

Rawls grinned. "It has been, hasn't it?"

Sally got up, gave Stone a hug and a kiss, then sat down again.

"When will we see you in New York?" Stone asked.

"We'll stop in for a few days on the way to Virginia, at the end of the season." Rawls got up and gave him a bearish hug. "Fly safe."

The Cessna did get off the ground, with runway to spare, and they dropped Carly off, then made for Rockport. As they lined up to land, they could see the Gulfstream waiting for them.

"I don't see a small plane," Primmy said.

"We're taking the large one, right there," Stone said, pointing.

"That beats the 1938 Ford," she said.

"You betcha."

END

October 21, 2020

Washington Depot, Connecticut

AUTHOR'S NOTE

I am happy to hear from readers, but you should know that if you write to me in care of my publisher, three to six months will pass before I receive your letter, and when it finally arrives it will be one among many, and I will not be able to reply.

However, if you have access to the Internet, you may visit my website at www.stuartwoods.com, where there is a button for sending me e-mail. So far, I have been able to reply to all my e-mail, and I will continue to try to do so.

Remember: e-mail, reply; snail mail, no reply.

When you e-mail, please do not send attachments, as I never open these. They can take twenty minutes to download, and they often contain viruses.

Please do not place me on your mailing lists for funny stories, prayers, political causes, charitable fund-raising, petitions, or sentimental claptrap. I get enough of that from people I already know. Generally speaking, when I get e-mail addressed to a large number of people, I immediately delete it without reading it.

Please do not send me your ideas for a book, as I have a policy of writing only what I myself invent. If you send me story ideas, I will immediately delete them without reading them. If you have a good idea for a book, write it yourself, but I will not be able to advise you on how to get it published. Buy a copy of *Writer's Market* at any bookstore; that will tell you how.

Anyone with a request concerning events or appearances may e-mail it to me or send it to: Putnam Publicity Department, Penguin Random House LLC, 1745 Broadway, New York, NY 10019.

Those ambitious folk who wish to buy film, dramatic, or television rights to my books should contact Matthew Snyder, Creative Artists Agency, 2000 Avenue of the Stars, Los Angeles, CA 90067.

Those who wish to make offers for rights of a literary nature should contact Anne Sibbald, Janklow & Nesbit, 285 Madison Avenue, 21st Floor, New York, NY 10017. (Note: This is not an invitation for you to send her your manuscript or to solicit her to be your agent.)

If you want to know if I will be signing books in your city, please visit my website, www.stuartwoods.com, where the tour schedule will be published a month or so in advance. If you wish me to do a book signing in your local-ity, ask your favorite bookseller to contact his Penguin rep-resentative or the Penguin publicity department with the request.

If you find typographical or editorial errors in my book and feel an irresistible urge to tell someone, please write to Sara Minnich at Penguin's address above. Do not e-mail your discoveries to me, as I will already have learned about them from others.

A list of my published works appears in the front of this book and on my website. All the novels are still in print in paperback and can be found at or ordered from any book-store. If you wish to obtain hardcover copies of earlier nov-els or of the two nonfiction books, a good used-book store or one of the online bookstores can help you find them. Otherwise, you will have to go to a great many garage sales.